TARGETED
FOR MURDER

ELIZABETH GODDARD

 HARLEQUIN® LOVE INSPIRED® SUSPENSE

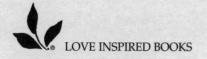

LOVE INSPIRED BOOKS

ISBN-13: 978-0-373-67782-5

Targeted for Murder

Copyright © 2016 by Elizabeth Goddard

www.Harlequin.com

Printed in U.S.A.

Trust no one.

But her father hadn't met Cooper Wilde when he'd said the words. Could he have known she'd be tracked into the heart of the wilderness? He'd given her no instructions on how, exactly, to stay hidden. All she had in her toolbox were implements to help her disappear.

And now, this one guy...

In a way, Cooper was the missing piece in her backpack. He was a weapon—the most capable person she'd ever met.

"You're risking your life by sticking around," she warned him.

"It wouldn't be the first time."

She averted her gaze. "Okay, if you're going to stick around–" Was she really saying this? "–then, you should know what you're getting into."

"That's all I'm asking."

Hadley climbed out. Cooper slid into the driver's seat. Shifting into gear, he steered the Jeep onto what barely counted as a road.

"I'm listening."

"What?"

"You were going to tell me what I'm getting into."

She sat for a moment, trying to collect her thoughts and figure out where to begin. He seemed to take her hesitation for reluctance, because he said, "I promise, you're safe with me. Your secret is safe with me."

Elizabeth Goddard is an award-winning author of more than twenty novels, including the romantic mystery *The Camera Never Lies*—winner of a prestigious Carol Award in 2011. After acquiring her computer science degree, she worked at a software firm before eventually retiring to raise her four children and become a professional writer. In addition to writing, she homeschools her children and serves with her husband in ministry.

Books by Elizabeth Goddard

Love Inspired Suspense

Wilderness, Inc.
Targeted for Murder

Mountain Cove
Buried
Untraceable
Backfire
Submerged
Tailspin
Deception

Freezing Point
Treacherous Skies
Riptide
Wilderness Peril

Visit the Author Profile page at Harlequin.com.

The Lord works righteousness and justice
for all the oppressed.
–Psalms 103:6

This story is dedicated to my parents, Barbara and Robin. Thank you for believing in me, for always encouraging me to reach for my dreams and to never give up.

Acknowledgments

This writing journey continues to amaze me as I travel roads that put me in contact with other writers, brilliant people whom I could never imagine I would brainstorm with on a monthly basis or meet with for a cup of coffee. Every time I spend time with writing friends, I come away realizing I'm a better writer for it. How truly blessed I am. So I want to say thanks to all my new writing buddies, and my longtime writing friends, as well. I couldn't have written so many stories without you! And a special thank-you to my dear friend, Shannon McNear, who now only lives five hours from me! Yes! We can meet once in a while for that cup of coffee in person. All these years of virtual chatting and God has blessed us with some face-to-face time outside of conferences. I appreciate my editor, Elizabeth Mazer, so much for allowing me to write such fun stories. And as always, my agent, Steve Laube, has been a rock for me, always there to encourage and support me when I need him.

ONE

Hadley Mason rubbed Butterfinger's soft fur, gently urging her neighbor's cat back inside. She'd agreed to feed and love on the tabby Persian for Teresa. An easy enough task, except for—a sneeze tickled her nose. Thankfully, Teresa would be home tomorrow.

Stepping into the carpeted hallway between the artist loft apartments, she pulled Teresa's door closed behind her and moved to her own.

Then froze in her steps.

Hers was ajar.

Frowning, she eased it all the way open and peeked inside, assessing the situation. She wasn't normally fearful but sometimes a girl had to be cautious, especially since she lived in the newly refurbished building that served as an artist community in a run-down part of town. Should she call the police? No…not yet. Not if there was any chance she might have accidentally left the door open herself.

But she really didn't think she had.

Stepping across the threshold, she glanced around, but saw nothing out of the ordinary. Her surreal paintings of animals in different environments covered the walls and would normally set her at ease.

But not now.

"Is someone here?"

"Hadley…" Coming from the dining room across the apartment, the voice sounded strained.

"Dad!" Hadley rushed through the foyer, past the kitchen and into the small dining alcove. With his business travel schedule, she wasn't supposed to see him again until Christmas in a couple of months. What a nice surprise. And she would have said as much except when she saw him sitting in the shadowed corner chair, she hesitated.

Something was wrong. Very wrong.

Her father wore his typical polished business suit but it was crumpled. His posture was slumped and his usual bright eyes were bloodshot as they studied her.

"Hadley, please sit down."

Fear slithered up her throat. Her father was all she had in the way of family. She never knew her mother, who'd died when she was born.

"What's going on?" She asked the question in a daze. "Why are you here?"

"Please." He gestured to the chair.

Hadley slowly obeyed, never taking her eyes from his pale features. The sweat beading his forehead. "Daddy," she whispered. "Tell me what's going on."

He leveled his pained gaze at her, struggling, battling with his words. Then he gave a subtle shake of his head. "I never meant for any of this to happen. For you to be dragged into this."

"Dragged into what? You're scaring me."

"There's not much time. I need you to listen carefully." He fought for breath. "I'm not who you think I am."

"What are you talking about?"

"I'm an agent...with the CIA."

Hadley frowned. Snorted a laugh. But that was preposterous. Wait...was he serious? "You're not a financial analyst?"

"No, that's just my cover."

She had to have misunderstood. "As in...wait... are you telling me that you're a spy?"

Unbelievable.

"Yes. I just wanted to make the world a safer place for you, sweetheart...but instead I've brought danger to your door. I'm so sorry." He slumped farther into the chair.

"Dad!" Hadley rushed to him and grabbed his

hand. "Should I call a doctor? What should I do? Tell me and I'll do it!"

"There isn't time."

"I don't understand."

She hated the tears blurring her vision. He wasn't making sense, so she needed to be the strong one—to get them through this.

But then he lifted his suit jacket away from his body, revealing a blood-soaked towel pressed against his chest and what would have been a crisp white shirt. Only then did Hadley notice the blood dripping to the Persian rug, which hid the crimson color well.

Her heart plummeted.

"I'm calling 911! You need an ambulance."

He grabbed her arm, held her tight, surprising her with his strength.

"You're going to bleed to death if I don't call for help."

"I've been shot, and there's nothing anyone can do for me now. I'm not going to make it."

She could staunch the flow, adding to his efforts, but he'd already lost so much blood. Now she understood better his deathly appearance… except for one thing.

"Why, Dad? Why did someone shoot you?"

"Someone put a contract out on me. Probably because of a past operation. And that's why I'm here. To warn you. You have to get out, Hadley. You have to hide."

"Me? What does this have to do with me?"

"You're my family. They have targeted you for elimination, too."

"But…why?"

"I don't have all the answers. My best guess? Revenge. I've done terrible things, Hadley, but sometimes the ends justifies the means, or at least I used to believe. But nothing is worth you getting hurt." He pointed to a backpack on the table. "That's for you."

Hadley pulled away from him and glanced at the pack, then back at her father. She was losing him.

God, help him. Help me!

"I don't care about the backpack, Dad. Let's get you out of here and somewhere safe—like the hospital."

Her mind was going in traitorous circles. She couldn't think clearly or straight. She was going into shock, herself. All Hadley knew was she must do something to save her father. She eyed her cell on the counter and started for it but he held her in place with a death grip, his expression painfully desperate.

"Listen," he hissed.

She didn't recognize her father. Who was this man?

"Pay attention. Your life depends on it. The

pack contains everything you'll need to disappear. Cash and a passport. A new identity. Don't use credit cards. Too easy to track. Grab your weapon. Take it with you…" Coughs spasmed from him, preventing him from saying more.

"What? I can't leave now! What about the gallery? Friday is my national debut." But as she said the words, she realized how shallow they sounded with what she was facing—her father's death. And the chance that his killer might come after her next.

"I know it's hard to take in all at once. I wanted to protect you. To keep you safe, but my world is…my world's colliding with yours. Lose your identity. Disappear. Hide and…"

Now her childhood was all making so much more sense. The Krav Maga weekends. The firing ranges. *Oh. My…*

Her father's head tilted forward. Hadley wanted to hug him, to keep him with her. "Daddy! Please, don't leave me. I love you."

His eyes were closed. Was he gone? Had she lost him? His lids fluttered, then he opened them again. "Leave now before he finds you and kills you. Trust no one. In the backpack—"

His eyes shut again and his head lobbed forward. Hadley sensed that he was gone. That her father no longer resided in this body. The thought overwhelmed her. She couldn't comprehend it all.

Gone.

Just like that.

He's gone.

Hadley dropped to her knees, pressed her face into her father's jacket and sobbed. "No, Daddy, no!"

His words echoed through her mind. *Leave now before he finds you and kills you.*

Was this real? Was any of this real? Hadley wiped her eyes and nose and tore herself away. She stood to her feet and grabbed her cell from the counter, then called 911. No matter what he said, she was calling the police. If she could even believe someone was after her, why couldn't the police help? Or the CIA, the people he worked for? The reason he was dead and she was in this predicament.

"What is your emergency?" the dispatcher answered.

"My father, he's been shot. He's…he's dead. And he says someone is trying to kill me, too."

The dispatcher asked for pertinent information that Hadley gave her. Afterward, she hung up and stared at her father's body, still in disbelief. This couldn't be happening. She paced the apartment, everything he'd just told her swirling through her mind in a vortex of confusion. Bile rose in her throat, moisture dampened her palms. She glanced at the backpack.

Leave now.

Trust no one.

Hadley snatched the bag and unzipped it. Shock rippled through her. Cash. There was so much cash. She'd never seen that much money in her life. Where had he gotten it? She glanced at him, then averted her gaze. She didn't want to think about her father as he was now in the chair. She didn't want that to be the prevailing memory of him. She tugged out the passport and saw her alias.

Megan Spears from Iowa?

Sirens rang out in the distance.

Panic cranked tighter around her throat. What would the police think when they found her with a bag of cash and a fake passport? Found her father dead? She glanced at her hands and her blouse. She was covered in his blood!

What do I do? What do I do?

Her entire life had just been ripped from under her. Her father's, too. She'd lost her father and possibly her identity. Add to that, if the police would suspect her of his murder first and if they found this bag of cash and a fake passport, they would have a lot of questions for her. She would have no answers. Would they even believe her?

Think. You have to think.

She had to hide the bag. But where?

Teresa's apartment.

Her friend wouldn't be back until tomorrow.

But if Hadley hid it and the police found it, then what would she say? She shook off the thought, refusing to let doubts freeze her into inaction.

She was running out of time and didn't have many choices.

Hadley snatched the bag and ran across the hallway. She unlocked the door, urged Butterfinger out of the way, and stashed the backpack at the top of the coat closet behind some boxes.

Oh, Daddy...

He could have gone to the hospital instead of coming to her apartment. If he had, he might have lived since the shot hadn't instantly killed him. He might have survived! But he chose to come here and warn her instead of getting treatment. He'd sacrificed his life to give her everything she would need to survive.

Hadley was the reason he was dead.

Just like she was the reason her mother had died.

But she couldn't think about that now. She had to focus on her father's purpose for coming here—to warn her. She had to think about his instructions.

Why didn't she leave, as he'd said? She knew she should, but she couldn't bring herself to give up everything she'd worked for and just walk away.

She glanced through the peephole just as a man

in a suit, wielding a weapon, burst through the door of her apartment. Her heart jumped up her throat. Hadley gasped for breath and pressed her back against the door.

He was not a police officer. Who was he? The man who killed her father? And now wanted to kill her?

She peered through the peephole again, fear and adrenaline rushing through her veins. She could see very little through the hole, but the man exited her apartment and closed the door. Holding a cell to his ear, he mumbled curses and other words she couldn't understand.

But she caught the last thing before he disappeared from view.

"...retaliation, payback. I have to clean up loose ends."

The words gripped her throat and squeezed. Hadley couldn't breathe.

Her father had been right. She couldn't trust anyone. Quickly Hadley went through Teresa's closet to find old clothes she could wear. She and Teresa were about the same size, and no way would she go back into her own apartment. After donning an old blue jean jacket over a fresh T-shirt and tugging a cap over her strawberry-blond hair, she crammed the bloody clothes she'd worn into a plastic garbage sack and then into the receptacle. Hadley didn't have time to properly dispose of the clothes. She wasn't even sure how.

After changing, she grabbed the backpack from the closet and climbed through the window and down the fire escape, grateful for old buildings.

In the alley, she had to hurry before the police arrived and cordoned off the space. The sirens grew louder. At the corner she caught a cab and asked the driver to take her to the airport. As it drove away from the curb, two police cruisers pulled up to the building.

An ambulance, too.

Took them long enough.

She sank into the seat of the cab, but she risked one more backward glance. The man who'd broken into her apartment spoke with the police. Hadley stared out the passenger window thinking about her father's instructions.

Trust no one.

Who was the man who'd come to her apartment? Was he acting alone, or were there other people after her? How could she protect herself if she didn't even know who she was up against? There had to be someone who could help her but her father hadn't given her names.

Whenever she was dealing with a problem, her first instinct was always to call her father. Not that she expected him to fix everything for her—

she just always felt better about things when she'd gotten his calm perspective and useful advice. Her heart clenched at the thought that she'd never be able to call him again. Tears spilled over her cheeks again. All these years, working as a struggling artist, and finally her work would debut on the national scene in a few days and what did any of it matter? Her father wouldn't be there at the opening reception.

If she didn't clear things up before the reception, neither would she be there. At the moment, she didn't even care.

She sniffled and turned her attention to the cabdriver who eyed her through the mirror. The windshield cracked and spidered at the same instant the driver's head jerked back, blood splattering the seat.

Tires screech and the cab accelerated, swerving precariously back and forth on the road. Everything happened too fast. Hadley's mind couldn't wrap around what was happening. The driver had been shot in the head. No one controlled the vehicle now.

She screamed and gripped the seat.

God help me!

Horns honked and metal crunched as vehicles crashed and twisted together.

The cab flipped two times and finally came to a crunching stop against a concrete divider.

Hadley groaned. It hurt to move, to breathe. She dragged in oxygen.

Squeezing her eyes shut, she shook her head, wanting to wake up from the worst dream of her life.

Leave now before he finds you and kills you.

He might have found her, but Hadley had to do what her father had instructed her to do and disappear. Lose the killer again before he killed her. Or her father's warning and his death would be for nothing.

But it was too late for the cabdriver.

He was gone. Hadley knew it.

Oh, God, help me. He has already killed someone else because of me.

Body aching and mind in shock, she grabbed the backpack and rolled out of her seat onto the concrete, hiding behind the cab as she carefully avoided the glass and twisted metal littering the road. Her pulse roared in her ears.

The cabdriver…dead… She could be next. And if she didn't get away from the people gathering to help, anyone near her could be killed.

Because of her.

Based on the trajectory of the bullet that killed the cabdriver, she figured the killer had shot from building on the southeast corner. Hadley used the wrecked cab as cover, she crawled over and into a narrow alley littered with garbage and smelling the same, then stood and ran the length of it until she came to another building. Hadley slipped around the corner. Leaning against the brick wall, she caught her breath as she listened. She dusted off the broken glass that clung to her clothes and tried to look normal so she could melt into the crowd. Not draw any attention.

Ignoring the pain and grief, she ran a few blocks and slipped down yet another alley and caught another cab.

"Take me to the airport." She didn't know where she would go, but she had to get out of town and fast.

Maybe she would simply ask for the next flight out.

Her father was dead. A cabdriver was dead because someone had put out a contract to kill her father, and now her.

Forget her national debut.

Forget her life. Her only focus should be on how to survive. Her father had given her the tools he believed she would need. A passport for one, but she couldn't imagine going overseas without a plan. She didn't know enough about international travel.

The spy world wasn't her world.

Until today, she'd had no idea it had been her father's.

Maybe she could hide in a city somewhere.

Get lost in the crowd, except she would be terrified of every single person who stood within an inch of her.

Her father might have made sure she could protect herself. But she couldn't protect herself against an unseen villain. Until she identified the man who would come to kill her...

Everyone was an assassin.

Southwest Oregon
4:00 p.m. Saturday

Cooper Wilde checked his footing on the rock that hung hundreds of feet above the Rogue River, then raised his binoculars. As he breathed in the scent of the old-growth forest and took in the vivid evergreens and rocky canyon, the tension in his neck drained away.

He loved it here.

A scream echoed from somewhere to his west. Cooper's gut tensed.

He heard the collective gasps of the women from the Rogue Valley Knitters and Knature Club behind him.

"What was that?"

"A woman screamed."

"Or a panther, a mountain lion. I hear they can sound like a woman screaming."

"Do you think a bear got her?"

"This is bear country, after all."

He zoomed the binoculars out, searching for something he could focus in on.

"Shh, quiet. Let him search in peace."

"There!" one of the women shouted. "I see something."

He eased away from the binoculars long enough to get a glimpse of where the river carved through the canyon, narrow and steep. That was a good mile from where they stood. He saw nothing to indicate a problem. But appearances could be deceiving.

Even though he considered this an undemanding hike, nothing was ever quite that easy in the Wild Rogue Wilderness, the region surrounding the government-protected portion of the Rogue River. This rugged landscape drew thousands of tourists and thrill seekers every year, many of whom took foolish risks.

Was that all the scream had been? A thrill seeker out for the time of her life?

Instinct told him no.

Frowning, he continued searching. "What did you see?"

"Someone running. The trees are thick so I only got a glimpse."

Then Cooper saw something, too, and pressed the binoculars tightly against his face. Through a copse of deciduous trees that had lost most of their leaves, he spotted a woman wearing a blue jean jacket, running for all she was worth.

Now... What are you running from? He searched behind her and saw a man carrying a weapon. Were they running together—maybe from a bear? Or was the man chasing the woman?

Indecision weighed on him.

Hesitation on his part could cost a life. Pain from the past echoed through his gut.

Cooper dropped the binoculars and peered back at his Wilderness, Inc., employee Melanie Shore. "Take them around on the short loop. I'll meet you at the trailhead if I can."

"Wait, what?"

"You'll get your hike, ladies, don't worry. But it's my job to make sure you're safe, too. Unless you're signing up for wilderness training today…"

"No, no," several replied.

He didn't blame them. They didn't have the training to help—he did. He'd served on Special Forces. A designated marksman. Although it had been five years, he'd never forgotten that familiar sixth sense that raised the hair on his arms and neck. It was what made him one of the top wilderness survival trainers. The reason his father had insisted his children enlist, get military training first.

Cooper didn't like the way his mind and body transformed into a creature of habit from his past, but if it meant saving a life, he'd go with it. He edged down until he got a grip on the rock and climbed down the cliff face until he could drop into the woods.

Feet on the ground, he pushed off and kept moving in stealth mode, his own weapon at the ready. He didn't like the hikers to see it. Didn't want to scare them, but in bear country and otherwise, he always carried.

Hearing the grunts of a struggle, he picked up the pace.

Near the rocky ledge overlooking the river, he saw the woman fighting with a man who looked more than capable of snapping her like a twig.

He let his body move into instinct mode—and charged.

TWO

He rushed forward while absorbing the scene before him, assessing and strategizing at the same time.

He had to get there before it was too late, even as he fought against the all-too familiar memories that threatened to shut him down.

Cooper focused on this one moment. This one life he could save.

The woman was young—late twenties, maybe—and had skills that had kept her alive this long. Maybe she'd even managed to disarm the man, since his weapon was no longer in sight.

Krav Maga.

He recognized the moves. She was good, but he could tell she grew tired, gasped for breath as her strength paled against the larger man. Bigger and stronger, the attacker looked like he worked out and fought every day for a living. He could already have killed her. Why was he toying with her?

Regardless of the reasons, his intentions were clear and he would overpower her soon.

All this Cooper took in on his approach. Before he reached the two, the man shoved her to the ground, straddled her and wrapped his hands around her throat.

Showtime.

Cooper made himself known, aimed his weapon at the man's head. "Let her go."

But the man ignored Cooper and continued to strangle her. The woman's eyes were already bloodshot.

"Let her go *now*, or I will shoot you." He fired off a warning shot. Still the man didn't let go.

Cooper didn't want to kill anyone. He'd seen too much blood already. Instead, he rushed him like a linebacker, barreling into him. Muscle jarred—steel swords clashing—as Cooper toppled the man, pushing him off the woman.

Together, they fell against the rocky ground, pebbles and sharp stones grinding into them. Cooper rolled and scrambled to his feet, raising his arm to strike the man across the head with the butt of his weapon, hoping to knock him unconscious. As his hand came down, the man thrust his arm up and gripped Cooper's wrist with surprising strength, preventing his strike.

He'd underestimated this man.

They rushed each other like two rutting elks.

The fight was on, and Cooper's weapon was tossed aside like an afterthought. A Green Beret in the army, he had his own set of hand-to-hand combat skills that included a variety of fighting styles. And right now, he was more than glad his exercise program continued to challenge him. Otherwise he would already be dead.

But he didn't practice this on a daily basis. Why should he? And now the man had him on the defensive, protecting all his vulnerable parts.

Eyes, neck, throat, solar plexus...

If he had any doubts before about his opponent's profession, they were long gone. He was certain this man was a hit man... No.

More than that.

An assassin.

Cooper had met his match and on his own home turf, no less.

Sweat trickled into his eyes and burned. He gasped for breath, ignored the pain. Ignored the frustration and let his instincts and fighting skills work for him. Cooper knew he was the weaker opponent in this match.

But he had an advantage somewhere.

What was it?

There had to be one.

They circled each other now, the man catching his breath as well. Something like the pleasure of a challenge glinted in the man's dark eyes.

"I haven't ever fought a mountain man." A scoffing laugh erupted.

Mountain man? So the man was trying to taunt him now?

"Then I have the advantage. I've fought plenty of killers. You're nothing special."

The other man just laughed, and pulled a knife from his pocket. "I've enjoyed sparring with you. But now the fun is over. This woman has already been too much trouble for me. Are you willing to lose your life for her?"

Cooper had no plans to die today, but who did? "I have every intention of making sure she's safe. That you don't succeed in killing her."

"Do you even know her?"

"Never seen her before in my life."

"A hero, then. Don't be a martyr, too—just walk away."

"Why are you trying to kill her?" Cooper asked, borrowing time. But the assassin was also stalling. For what purpose, Cooper couldn't know.

"I tell you what…" He gestured behind him to the cliff's edge. "You toss her down the cliff for me and I'll let you live."

The man was twisted in ways Cooper didn't want to linger on.

But he'd given Cooper an advantage, sparking a memory that allowed anger and rage from the past to drive him, empower him. He'd watched his brother throw himself over. Commit suicide.

Cooper hadn't been able to stop him. Now was the moment he could let go and unleash the beast.

Letting that memory fuel him, Cooper charged the man and quickly disarmed him of the knife. They rolled until they were at the cliff's edge. Doubt crawled over Cooper. Would the assassin push him off the ledge to his death? Take Cooper with him when he fell?

Then the woman was there, pounding on the assassin entangled with Cooper, using martial arts again until the man freed himself from them—but then lost his footing. He hung on to the gnarled roots growing from the rocky ledge as he clung for his life.

Cooper reached for him. "Give me your hand. I'll pull you up."

Fear didn't grip the man like Cooper would have expected. Instead anger and hate filled the man's gaze. Determination marked his features, and he made no move to accept Cooper's help. Cooper reached, grabbing the man's arm. In this position, the man could take him with him if he chose to fall and drag Cooper along.

What am I doing?

But even if the man was an assassin, Cooper couldn't stand by and watch another man die like this. And anyway, he still wanted answers.

"Why kill her? What's she to you? Who are you?" In his peripheral vision, he could see that she stood back and away from the edge, eerily silent. She had to already know the answer.

A smirk lifted the man's lips. "It's just business. If I die, it's only a matter of time before another will come."

Then, he twisted out of Cooper's grip and dropped, his body falling hundreds of feet toward the rocky Rogue River rapids below.

Cooper couldn't bring himself to watch, this image melding with the other of his brother's fall to his death.

But now was not the time to lose himself in memories or guilt. Not when the woman was still there, with possibly another killer on her trail.

Hadley pressed her hand against her midsection, trying to comprehend what had just happened. Cold laced the wind that rushed over her and rustled the trees like it was any other day. As though none of what she'd experienced had happened.

The man who'd fought with the assassin turned away from the cliff's edge and faced her, his broad shoulders rising and falling as he caught his breath— *Or maybe in disbelief.*

He tugged off his ripped jacket. Sweat darkened the back of his shirt, torn at the arm.

If only she could get the assassin's last words out of her head.

It's just business. If I die, it's only a matter of time before another will come.

Nausea roiled. She'd done the best she could to disappear. Now what? Where did she go?

Her eyes rose to the face of the man who'd inserted himself into her fight. It was caked with blood and dirt, as was his shaggy brown hair. His steel-blue eyes stared at her. He appeared as shocked as she was from the events of the last few moments.

But he was still alive.

She took in his sturdy six-foot form. He didn't look much older than her. Early thirties, maybe? He was definitely well-trained. He'd somehow survived fighting with the assassin sent to kill her.

Her relief palpable, she almost cried.

"Are you okay?" His voice was gentler than she had expected.

But what must he think of her? "No."

This wasn't over.

I have to know.

Hadley rushed over to the edge. She had to see the body. Had to see that he was dead.

The man caught her at the waist and pulled her back from the edge.

"Whoa. What are you doing?"

She twisted in his arms. Powerful arms. "I have

to see that he's dead! To make sure he's gone."
She sounded like a crazy person. She didn't recognize her own voice.

"He's dead."

"Let me go!"

When he relinquished his hold, oddly, Hadley almost wished he hadn't. She crept to the edge and vertigo hit her. She forced herself to look down, searching, but when she swayed on her feet, he gently gripped her arm and tugged her back.

"I don't see him."

"The river took him."

"Then he could still be alive."

"No, he couldn't."

"But you don't know that."

"Look. He's dead, all right?"

"I don't know." Wouldn't she feel safer if he was dead? Instead, she didn't feel safe at all. "He seemed so invincible. I can't believe the fall would kill him. Is there a chance that he could have survived, no matter how small?"

He produced a sigh as if giving up. "Yes. There's always a chance. Of course, there is. It's doubtful, but anything is possible."

Okay, so there was that possibility. And another equally as terrifying.

Hadley opened her eyes. "You heard him. It doesn't matter if he's dead. Someone else will come."

Deep lines creased his forehead. He studied her

as if he were sifting through her insides, look-ing for anything good and coming up short. Now she'd done it.

Why had she blurted that out?

"Who was he? Why does he want to kill you?"

"I don't know."

Squeezing her eyes shut, she thrust her hands in her hair and fisted them, wanting this to end. Wanting to curl into a ball and cry. But that wasn't an option.

She couldn't afford to reveal anything but her strong side. Hated that this stranger saw her mo-ment of weakness. Except she needed this chance to release the anguish.

Though her knees shook, limbs trembled, she wouldn't cry. She wouldn't release the racking sobs building up inside.

She needed to force strength into her shaky legs and walk out of here. Grab her gear at the place she'd rented—a remote cabin that the killer should never have been able to find. If she hadn't seen him from a distance, she wouldn't have been able to make a run for it into the wilderness.

That run for her life had only gained her a few moments, yet that had been enough time for an unexpected warrior to appear and fight on her behalf.

Drawing in a calming breath, she opened her eyes. The man was grimacing, and his own eyes were closed. Hadley focused on him instead of herself. He must have been stabbed or injured in some way.

"Where are you hurt?"

He opened his eyes. She could clearly see the pain in them, but it wasn't physical. It looked like something more. Something deeper. "I asked if you're hurt," she repeated.

"Not in any way that can be fixed. What about you?"

She could have answered in the same way. "I'm okay."

"Then let's get you out of here."

He grabbed her arm, but Hadley had no intention of going anywhere with him. "Let me go."

He did as she asked.

She sucked in a breath. "Thank you for helping me. You saved my life."

"You were holding your own there."

"Barely. He would have killed me if you hadn't come. Now, if you know what's good for you, you'll get back to whatever you were doing and I'll just be on my way."

"Hold on." He caught her again, and this time tightened his grip. "You sure you don't know who he was or why he was trying to kill you? That man wasn't just anyone. He was a trained killer. I want some answers. And you can't just run off. We have to report what happened. A man is dead."

Trust no one.

She couldn't trust the police. But how did she explain this to her rescuer? He'd helped her... but she couldn't rely on him. And even if she had been willing to trust him, she had no right to pull him into her troubles. It would be better and safer for them both if she pushed him away.

Hadley stared at his hand on her arm. "Like I said, if you know what's good for you, you'll let me go now. You know I can fight you if I have to."

Immediately he released her. "I'm just trying to help. Let's call the sheriff. I need to report what happened. That...someone fell over a cliff." A deep agony edged his tone.

Hadley searched the woods for the direction she should hike. She didn't like the way he was hanging on, trying to prevent her from escaping, though she could tell he meant well.

"I can't wait around."

The man stiffened at that. "Look, I'm no idiot. I know I just fought with an assassin, and likely what's going on here is more than a backcountry sheriff can handle, but there are still channels to go through."

Hadley had slowly started putting distance between them. The sooner she left him behind the better. But he seemed to be on to her plan and stepped forward. He held his palms out. "Don't I have the right to know if by helping you that I've involved myself in something? What if someone is going to come looking for me now, too?"

His words reached across the way and grabbed her throat. Squeezed a few tears up into her eyes. Her father. The cabdriver. No more. No one else could die.

"That's why I have to get out of here. Just stay away from me!" Hadley turned and ran toward the deeper woods.

"Look, what's your name?" he called. "At least give me that. I'll go first. My name is Cooper Wilde. I own and run Wilderness, Inc."

She slowed then. Turned to face him. *Please, don't tell me any more.* She couldn't get further entangled with him.

Hadley had a few ideas of what sort of business that might be, but she wasn't sure what name she could give him. Her alias? Or her real name? "Look. You're a good guy, I can see that. But I need to disappear. I don't know you and I can't trust you. I can't trust anyone. I don't want to get you involved and risk getting you killed because of me."

"I'm already involved. I just dispatched the bad guy, in case you hadn't noticed." His voice turned curt.

Sounded like he was running out of patience.

"And don't make me have to fight the good guys, too. Okay?" Hadley started back the way she'd come, pushing through the brush, reminiscing each terrifying moment she'd spent trying to outsmart, outrun and out-hide a man who was trying to kill her, all because of her father.

Even he hadn't known who was targeting them. Could only guess at a revenge contract.

What would it hurt to have someone to lean on? Someone she could trust?

But she didn't know who that would be.

She glanced over her shoulder and didn't see Cooper following her. The sharp pain of disappointment stabbed her, but she couldn't let herself depend on anyone else.

To depend on someone else could be deadly.

THREE

Thirst drove her worse than her exhaustion as she hiked every miserable mile back to the rental cabin. This time, she failed to even bother to search the area for anyone waiting there to kill her.

With not one ounce of energy left, she couldn't bring herself to care.

Finally, there it was, tucked away in the greenery like something from a postcard. Seeing the cabin revived her. There, she could sit. Massage her aching feet. Drink a gallon of water.

She crept onto the porch. Cautiously, she pushed through the door, thinking back to that moment when she'd spotted the man who meant to kill her. She'd seen it in his stance, his prowling around the cabin, and then in his eyes.

But he wasn't a problem right now. Even if he'd survived the fall, he had to be badly injured, and would need a recovery period before he could attack again. If someone else came for her, she was counting on that taking some time. Either way, she had a little breathing room—which was a very good thing. She needed a chance to catch her breath. Get her feet under her.

Hadley dropped in the old rickety chair in the corner and hugged herself, her insides turning over. She gulped the old musty air in the room. If she wasn't safe here, in the middle of this wild backcountry—then where could she go?

But she had to leave now, because that man— Cooper Wilde—would bring the local authorities to her door. The sheriff's office had to investigate the report of the death of an assassin and his attempt to kill Hadley. Then she would be questioned. And if they discovered she had a fake passport and a bag of cash, they would get even more suspicious if not take her into custody. She could already be wanted for questioning in her father's death, especially since she ran from the scene after calling the police to begin with.

And once in custody, she would be an easy target for a contract killer.

No. She couldn't let that happen.

She had to find a solid hiding place or keep moving, at least until she knew who was behind this. So far, she'd been simply trying to survive. She hadn't had time to worry about discovering who was after her. Yet she had a feeling none of this would end until the person who wanted her dead was truly unmasked.

But that was a problem for another day. Today, her focus was on staying alive.

Drawing on strength she didn't feel, Hadley gathered the few items she'd purchased in Medford. She thought back to how she'd gotten to Gideon, Oregon, the small town smack in the middle of the Wild Rogue Wilderness.

Once she had arrived at the Portland airport, she'd learned from the agent at the ticketing counter that the next available flight was to Medford, Oregon. Hadley had almost gasped. That was perfect. From there she could drive to Gideon. Hadn't she always wanted to spend time in the Wild Rogue Wilderness? She could hide out and paint.

But her attempt to salvage her dream hadn't lasted long. She hadn't been here a day when the assassin had shown up to kill her.

She grabbed the backpack with the cash and her new identity. How had he tracked her? Had he known the name on her passport? If so, then she'd need a new one. But Hadley didn't have a clue how to change her identity.

With a quick intake of breath, she let the pack slip to the floor and thought back to those last moments with her father. She couldn't get them out of her head.

He'd taught her skills. Yes. The self-defense training had kept her alive. But why hadn't he taught her other skills—like how to hide, or create a false identity? She had no experience with deception—but her father, it seemed, was a master. He wasn't the man she had thought he was. There was so much more she wished she had known, and now she never would.

Had he lied about her mother, too? Hadley had been told that her parents had lived happily in that small house on the Oregon Coast until her mother died in childbirth. What was the real story behind the house where they spent Christmas every year? Was it all a sham?

Oh, God. What do I do now? This wasn't supposed to happen. Why couldn't You at least have let my father live, so we could have run away together? He could have protected me.

She had to pull herself together to survive another day.

Hadley could do this. She must if she wanted to live.

She picked up the pack and pulled it on again. If only she had the luxury of telling her story to the sheriff like a normal person experiencing a normal crime.

But there wasn't anything about this situation that was normal. Her father had said she should trust no one and she would adhere to his advice for now. There was nothing anyone could do for her, not even Cooper Wilde, the assassin killer.

She thought back to the wild intensity in his eyes, the visible strength of his body springing into action. A protector on steroids.

He had skills. Part of her regretted leaving him so abruptly. But surely it was for the best.

A faint noise, the hint of a sound, drew her attention. She held her breath and listened.

Not-so-subtle footfalls clunked on the porch.

Her biggest regret was that she hadn't had a chance to grab her weapon like her father had told her. Nor had she had a chance to buy a new one.

She'd give anything for that protection now.

Clunk, clunk, clunk.

If it was another assassin, he could shoot her right through the wall. Fear gripped her. She held still and kept quiet. She wouldn't give herself away if it weren't already too late.

Someone knocked. "Are you there? It's Cooper."

Sweat bled from her palms. If only they were wrapped around her Glock.

Trust no one.

Never mind this man had saved her life. Maybe he was a threat to her, maybe he wasn't. Right now, what bothered her was that he'd found her too quickly and easily. Why was it so hard to disappear?

* * *

"What do you want?"

Cooper scraped a hand down his face, wishing he'd had a chance to clean up.

"To talk. That's all."

"Is the sheriff with you?"

He leaned against the door, wanting to break through, but that would send her running quicker than anything. "No."

Not yet.

He'd called once he'd gotten a signal but there wasn't a deputy on duty for another four hours. The county seat where the sheriff's office resided was sixty miles from Gideon. Still, the dispatcher said she'd make some calls and see if she could get someone out to Cooper.

Good thing the town wasn't under siege. The joy of living in an actual designated wilderness region.

Never mind the location was so remote mail arrived via boat service. Oh well, if it was good enough for novelist Zane Grey, who wrote in a nearby cabin, it was good enough for Cooper.

"I don't have time," she said.

That's right. She was in a hurry to run away.

"Could you at least open the door?"

The door creaked open slowly. Her posture was defensive. She would to fight her way out of here if he forced her.

He threw his hands up in surrender. "Whoa. I'm not the bad guy here, remember?"

Her wary expression didn't change, but she stood aside, albeit reluctantly, then waved him in.

Cooper shut the door behind him.

"I can't stay here. If there's someone coming for me, I need to disappear. You're holding me up."

"I thought you should know it'll be a while before anyone shows up to check on the guy who went into the river."

Her face scrunched up. "So you *did* call the sheriff."

"I tried. But deputies run thin around here." He wouldn't go into population to square mileage.

"Thanks, but you're not helping. Why did you come again? To hold me for the law?"

Cooper wanted to kick himself. "Just trying to do the right thing."

"You mean you were trying to cover yourself."

"And you. But hey, I don't even know your name."

"Megan Spears from Iowa."

Cooper frowned. Scratched his head. Megan Spears from Iowa? Right. After refusing to tell him anything earlier, she was suddenly willing to share her full name and where she was from? Unlikely. It had to be a false identity. But it was better than just calling her "the woman" in his head. "It's nice to meet you, Megan Spears from Iowa."

Megan Spears from Iowa sagged, probably just realizing her *faux paus*.

"So you don't want to give me your real name. It's okay."

What am I getting myself into? I don't have anything left to give, especially to help a girl in this much trouble.

"I need to disappear and yesterday." Her words were strong, but they belied her appearance— scratched, bleeding and exhausted.

She tried to push past him.

"Wait," he said. "I can help. I teach survival training. I have a military background. Just…let me help you."

Hadley shrank if only a millimeter. "I'm listening."

A half grin cracked into her lips. But why was she staring? "What?"

"You have a gash on your forehead. You're bloody and bruised and you don't even care. I saw how you fought. I think… I think I could believe your background."

So she had trust issues, huh? Well, with trained killers after her, he could hardly blame her. Cooper had just offered her the first real chance to believe someone in a while, it would seem.

Cooper offered his own half grin. Except his smile wiped away the moment.

Her lips flattened. "It makes no difference. I need to leave."

"Do you know where you're going next? Where to hide?"

"It's none of your business." This time Megan pushed by him and he let her.

The sun was setting and the air grew chilled. "If you need to hide, I can help you. Don't you get it?"

She whirled on him. "Why would you help me? You don't even know me."

He'd been asking himself that same question, and wondering if he even still had what it took to deal with this kind of life-and-death situation, that is, after failing so miserably. "I've trained my whole life to help people. It's what I do. My business is about training people to survive. So I recognize when someone is desperate and needs help. I can't turn my back on you. I won't."

His reasons went deeper, much deeper, he suddenly realized. He hadn't seen how desperate his brother was until it was too late and he'd taken that suicide plunge. That had shaken Cooper's confidence to the core. Even his father had blamed him. Hadley was desperate for far different reasons—he could see that and had no excuse this time. Without Cooper's help she would die.

Now, how did he convince her to let him help?

"The kind of survival assistance I need goes far beyond what you train people for."

"How do you know?"

She cocked a brow.

"And *you're* up to the task?" he asked.

She turned her back on him and started for the old Jeep Wrangler soft top.

Cooper followed. He'd been on foot all day and had found his way here, trailing her from a distance.

How did he convince her? "How about just for the night? Just so you have time to think and rest. You can stay at the apartment above the storefront for Wilderness, Inc., in Gideon."

"Whose apartment is it?"

He'd be embarrassed to admit it was his, once she saw it, but she'd figure it out soon enough. He'd have to be up-front with her from the start. One small white lie and she would run. "Mine. I'll sleep in the office downstairs until you figure out your next step."

"How do I know you're not trying to keep me here until the sheriff comes?"

Another good question. That hadn't been his intention.

"You want to know if the man is dead, don't you? Getting the sheriff involved will mean people searching for a body down the river." That was the wrong thing to say—she wanted fewer people involved, not more. "He doesn't have to know about you. I'll tell him I saw a woman getting attacked, I fought with a man and the woman disappeared. That's all."

"So you want to do the right thing and call the sheriff but you're not going to tell him the whole truth?"

"I will tell him, but not until I know you're safe." *What are you getting yourself into, Cooper Wilde?*

But he knew the sheriff would understand after he told him everything. This woman could be dead by the morning if he didn't find a way to help her tonight.

"I'm sorry, but my fa— I can't trust anyone. Not even the police."

"You're not from here, so there's no reason to believe the sheriff is connected to any of the people after you, right?"

"No, but he might tell other people. I don't want any information about me to get out."

"He won't—not if I ask him not to."

She looked skeptical. "How well do you know this sheriff?"

"I've known him for years."

"And you trust him?"

Did he? But Cooper hesitated too long and she

huffed her way past him and climbed into her old clunker.

Helping someone survive had never been this grueling.

FOUR

Hadley jammed the key in the ignition.

Cooper didn't follow her. He'd let her go. For that, she was grateful. So why did disappointment swirl around inside?

She couldn't have another death on her conscience. She'd have to keep her distance from everyone until this was over. If it ever was.

Except how could she really do this all on her own?

She needed someone to help, but it was too risky to trust anyone, on all fronts.

The engine turned over once. Twice. Then died. She tried again. Good thing she wasn't running from an assassin at this moment. Why had she bought such an old vehicle? With the cash in her bag, she could have bought something new and sturdy.

She was aware of Cooper watching her in the waning light of day, hands on his hips. Why didn't he just go away? He had no idea. *No. Idea.* What he'd be getting into if he stayed.

She squeezed the steering wheel, frustration building in her chest. She couldn't accept his offer of help.

Could she?

Exhaustion overwhelmed her. She eyed the cabin with longing—but there was no way she could spend the night there.

How had that man found her? He'd said someone else would come after her. Even if she ran, would they find her next hiding place just as easily? If she didn't figure out this most basic problem of how to cover her tracks—and soon—she was dead.

Cooper knocked on the window.

She jumped. Too tired to stay alert, she hadn't realized he'd approached the Jeep. Her inattention could have been deadly.

He stared down at her, waiting. The vehicle was so old, she had to physically roll down the window. It squeaked with each crank of the handle.

He folded his arms against the window frame and leaned in, too close for comfort. An image of him fighting the assassin—like some fine-tuned war machine—accosted her. Something about him, something feral in his presence, made her insides hum. Would it be so wrong to rely on him a little? She didn't have to trust him with everything…well, just her life.

Trust no one.

But her father hadn't met Cooper Wilde when he'd said the words. Could he have known she'd be tracked into the heart of the wilderness? He'd given her no instructions on how, exactly, to stay hidden. All she had in her toolbox were implements to help her disappear.

And now, this one guy…

In a way, Cooper was the missing piece in her backpack. He was a weapon. And from what she'd seen so far, he appeared to be the most capable person she'd ever met.

"You're risking your life by sticking around."

"It wouldn't be the first time."

She averted her gaze. "Don't you get it?"

When she looked back at him, he proffered that crazy grin. He had some charm about him, but she didn't think that was his intention. He came across as more of a warrior.

"Okay, if you're going to stick around—" was she really saying this? "—then you should know what you're getting into."

"That's all I'm asking."

Hadley climbed out. Cooper slid into the driver's seat.

"What are you doing?"

"Let's get out of here and you can tell me while I drive."

"Where are you taking me?"

"Anywhere would be safer than this cabin."

Hadley ran around and climbed into the passenger seat. "Can you get it started?"

He turned the key. Kept trying until the engine turned over. Then smiled at her. "I have the right touch."

"You just tried longer than I did, that's all."

"Like I said. The right touch."

Shifting into gear, he steered the Jeep onto what barely counted as a road. Hadley felt like she was handing her life over to a complete stranger. She held on to the handgrip, feeling the strain of the geriatric vehicle as it bumped and jolted over the potholes and through the darkening forest.

"I'm listening."

"What?"

"You were going to tell me what I'm getting into."

She sat for a moment, trying to collect her thoughts and figure out where to begin. He seemed to take her hesitation for reluctance, because he said, "Megan Spears from Iowa… I promise, you're safe with me. Your secret is safe with me."

"Okay, well for starters, my real name is…" Should she do it? Should she jump in with both feet? But Hadley needed to tell someone. "My name is Hadley Mason."

He glanced at her intermittently, but then focused back on the hazardous road out. Her cabin hadn't been too far from the nearest town and soon enough, they saw the lights flickering between the trees, dotting the forest like stars in the sky.

Gideon, Oregon—a quiet, remote historical town smack in the middle of the Wild Rogue Wilderness.

Cooper urged the old Jeep into the shadows behind a two-story home near the center of the tiny town. He turned off the ignition, then shifted in the seat to give her his full attention.

Oh, boy.

"What are you doing? Why are we…parked in the shadows?"

"This is the back of my business. The house is both storefront and home." He gestured to the second story. "That's the apartment, should you choose to stay. I'm parked in the shadows so nobody will see or bother us. I didn't want to assume, though, that you had agreed to stay. I'm still waiting to hear your story."

"Yeah, and after you hear it I'm waiting to have that invitation withdrawn."

"Not likely."

Hadley drew in a breath and spilled everything that had happened this morning. She shared about the passport but stopped just short of telling him about all the cash in her backpack. Money changed people. And if he chose to steal from her, what recourse did she have? He knew she didn't want to go to the police.

The events of her day seemed like a lifetime ago but it hadn't been twelve hours. The words made her sound crazy.

"And now, here I am. With you. But you don't have to be involved. You can let me walk away."

Hadley waited for him to respond.

But Cooper Wilde just stared at her.

Right. Why had she hoped he wouldn't think she was as crazy as she sounded? Oh, yeah, because he'd fought with her assassin. He had some evidence she spoke the truth.

"Are you going to say anything?"

He blew out a long pent-up breath he'd obviously held through her entire story.

Cooper scraped a hand over his face. Again. At the look on her face, he realized his action hadn't exactly conveyed confidence. He was doing a poor job of reassuring her. She'd run if he didn't respond right away and with the correct answer. But he had no idea what to say. How to respond.

That was one wild story.

So he just said, "Give me a second to think. That was…a lot."

Still, he knew she had to be telling the truth.

"You don't believe me."

"I do, actually." And wished he didn't. "Remember, I fought with the guy trying to kill you."

"That doesn't mean you have to believe the rest of the story."

"No, but it sounds right. He wasn't the typical thug one would run into around here." Or anywhere else. Nor was he a backwoods drug runner. Clearly she was involved in something high level. The only thing that wasn't certain was whether she was lying about being an innocent victim— but his gut told him she was telling the truth.

"Well, I guess this is goodbye." She opened her door and stepped out.

"Wait a minute." Cooper jumped out and ran around the vehicle. Stepping in her path, he held out his hands like he tried to calm a skittish mare. "Where are you going to go? You can't run from this on your own."

"What do you suggest I do? Wait for the sheriff? This is above his pay grade." Hadley started pacing, the dim light from his apartment above lighting her path. "I didn't ask for any of this." She stopped and stared at him. "And neither did you."

Her curly, strawberry-blond hair askew, weary

didn't begin to describe her. She appeared fragile and yet he'd seen her combat skills firsthand. Knew she was physically strong. Believed there had to be something strong inside, too, that had kept her alive. She'd said her father had taught her the skills. He must have suspected this day might come. What had he done that resulted in this happening to his daughter?

"I'm sorry about your father," he said. "He obviously loved you. Wanted you to be safe."

She hung her head. "Thanks."

"What do you do for living, Hadley?"

"Why does that matter?"

"I'm forming a plan. Just work with me."

"I'm an artist—a painter. I have a following on Etsy that pays the bills. I'm slowly building my career with exhibitions in small galleries and museums and a few commissioned pieces. But this coming Friday I have an exhibit that will propel me onto the national scene. I'm making my big debut, you could say. Or I was, until all this happened."

An artist? He hadn't expected that. The news left him unsettled. Disturbed.

Cooper squeezed his eyes closed, remembering. His brother Jeremy had been an artist before he committed suicide. Cooper caught himself. Now wasn't the time to relive the horror or wallow in the guilt. He focused back on Hadley.

Were those tears shimmering in her eyes? She blinked them away. Back at the cabin, before daylight had faded, he'd noticed the greens and golds swirling in her irises.

Cooper had to stay on task.

If only something about Hadley and her situation didn't tug at his heart, tipping it a little bit in her favor. He gently pushed the feeling back. He was nowhere near ready to let himself care about someone. But that didn't mean he wouldn't help a person in trouble, especially this kind of inescapable deadly trouble.

He was all over making sure she stayed safe. Who was Cooper Wilde if he couldn't protect someone in her position? His business, Wilderness, Inc., would mean nothing.

"I was thinking you could stay in the apartment. Work in the back office, if you want. Was hoping you'd say you were a bookkeeper." He tossed her an apologetic shrug. "That would keep you safe and out of sight until we can form a plan."

Find the source of this contract and end it for good.

"You'd want me to stay long enough to work here? That's crazy. Haven't you heard anything I've said? I can't stick around here when someone's after me. What if something happens to you because of me? I can't be responsible."

"Let me worry about myself." Cooper was all for justice. Unfortunately he wasn't sure Hadley was going to get it the usual way. There was no one else he could trust with her safety, not even the authorities.

He thought back to her story about the official-looking man who burst through the door of her apartment, weapon drawn, before the police even arrived. Then how she'd seen him speaking with the police when she left, confirming to Hadley the man worked in some official capacity. But the fact that he'd mumbled to himself about taking care of loose ends raised the hairs on Cooper's neck.

No wonder she was scared to trust anyone, even the police. And if the CIA was involved, all bets were off.

She watched him now, waiting on him to lead on if he meant his invitation. The night closed in around them, and Hadley shivered. What kind of guy was he to keep her out here waiting? And what kind of guy was he if he didn't use every resource he had to help her?

"I have connections. Someone who can help me find out who is after you." Someone he didn't want to contact. He'd wait until there was no other choice.

Hadley studied him.

First things first. "Let me show you the apartment. You can crash there, and make a decision in the morning, if you're not ready tonight."

She sagged. "Honestly, I can't think straight. I haven't eaten. I've been running all day. I'm fried."

Cooper didn't want to say he was counting on that. "Let me show you my humble abode."

He grabbed her backpack from the Jeep, locked it up—as if that mattered much—and together they hiked the outside stairs up to the apartment. He shoved the door open. It hadn't been locked. He'd never had a need to lock the door.

Until today.

She eyed him before walking into his apartment. He'd left a light on in the corner. Hadley stood in the middle of the small efficiency apartment and looked around.

"It's not much," Cooper said apologetically.

Her gaze landed on a painting of old-town Gideon, then drifted back to him. "Thank you," she barely croaked out.

Cooper had the sudden urge to reach out and grab her, draw her to him. Hold and comfort her. He fisted his hands against the unwelcome emotions, preventing them from acting out his desires.

No. No, no. He wouldn't let her crawl under his skin. He was just doing his job as a good person. One who knew something of the world. "You're welcome. The shower and bath are through there. I'll see if I can find something for you to eat, and then I'll crash in the office downstairs."

"My father told me not to trust anyone, Cooper. Anyone. And here… I'm letting myself trust you."

He swallowed the knot in his throat. Determination filled him to see this through with her. To the end. He was nothing if not committed to his missions, if not loyal to his assignments. He might try to think of Hadley as just an assignment, but she was much more. She was a person who mattered. A beautiful woman who had fought an assassin and survived. And Cooper would listen to the alarms resounding in his brain and stop his heart from connecting, nip this attraction before it started. Keeping her safe was what mattered. He could do that and keep his heart in line at the same time because he had the training.

De opresso liber.

Liberator of the oppressed was the Green Beret motto. Never mind he hadn't been able to save his brother from his internal torments.

"I'm not just anyone. You can count on me to do my best to help you, Hadley."

That seemed to satisfy her. She grabbed her backpack along with another small bag, then closed the door to the bedroom. Cooper brushed off the faint stirrings in his heart and searched his refrigerator, scolding himself for not keeping it reasonably stocked. Eggs. That was all he had. It would have to do.

While he whipped up scrambled eggs, minus butter or bacon on the side, he considered all his options.

God, how do I keep her safe? How do I stop this contract out on her?

First thing he should do starting tomorrow was give her a few wilderness survival pointers, in case she really had to disappear on her own. In case the worst happened and Cooper was taken out. He couldn't discount that possibility.

Then there was the fact that even if that bad guy was dead, another would come after her. The next attempt on her life might be the last if they succeeded. The new guy might not be interested in playing first.

So Cooper needed to keep her good and hidden.

And he needed to warn the others around him, his family and employees, to keep an eye out for anyone who acted suspicious.

He finished the eggs and dumped them on a plate and set it with a fork on the small table. Poured a glass of water. Grabbed the salt-and-pepper shaker and searched for a paper towel. A napkin. Something to show her he was civilized.

The fixings were slim around here. If he were looking to impress her, he was sure to fail. Good thing he wasn't looking.

A knock came at his door.

That would be either Deputy Callahan or…

Someone to kill Hadley.

FIVE

A hot shower had never felt so good. Too bad she couldn't stay there forever. When she was done cleaning up, Hadley dug in the bag for the few extra items of clothing she'd bought and found something to wear. She changed into a clean T-shirt and pulled on sweats, which she'd sleep in tonight. She tugged a hoodie over towel-dried hair, her bruised muscles and sore body aching with the effort.

Too bad the shower hadn't washed away the treachery of the day. Today had been the worst day of her life, and it seemed there was no end in sight. How would Hadley know when it was over? How could she find out about the contract on her life?

Was she wrong to take Cooper up on his offer? Was she too naive to see that she couldn't trust him? And even if she could trust him, she had to remember that she was putting him in danger and he could die, too, because of her.

Her thoughts shifted away from her plight when her stomach rumbled at the aroma of eggs, and her heart melted, just a little, at the idea of Cooper cooking for her—taking care of her. She opened the door and walked into the small kitchenette to see the plate of food set out for her. Water, utensils and a napkin. But no Cooper? The chair scraped when she tugged it from the table to sit. The food would get cold if she didn't eat it. Cooper had more to take care of than her, so she wouldn't worry about him.

Hunger overtook her. Hadley ate the eggs and could have easily licked the plate but she remembered her manners, even though she was alone. She finished off the water and went to the kitchen to get more.

Images flashed from her terrifying ordeal. A shudder ran over her. She was alone in this apartment. She didn't even know who this guy was. Not really. But she'd made up her mind that she had to take shelter here at least for the night.

If only it weren't so eerie and quiet. Hadley had never lived in fear before. Didn't want to now, but she had no control over her trembling hands. Her spiking pulse.

Was she having some sort of PTSD episode? After what she'd been through, she wouldn't be surprised. She didn't want Cooper to see her like this.

Where had he gone? Hadley decided he must have gone down to his office to sleep. She locked the dead bolt on the door that led out back, surprised he hadn't done that for her when he'd left. The door that opened up this apartment to the rest of the house only had a privacy lock on the knob. Anyone could open this with a kitchen utensil. She would have appreciated if he'd at least told her he was leaving for the night.

Guilt suffused her. Who was she to run this guy out of his apartment? To mess up his life?

God, I don't know what else to do.

Cooper had been a lifesaver for her today—literally—and she shouldn't be ungrateful. But she had no real way to show her gratitude. If anything, just being around him was punishing him by putting him at risk.

And with the thought it suddenly occurred to her she should watch the news to see if there was anything about her father. Murders occurred every day and not all of them were reported on the news. But there wasn't a television in the apartment, anyway. Obviously, the man didn't spend his time here except to sleep and fix some eggs in the morning. She tried to search the internet on her phone for some news, but the signal wasn't that great and she couldn't pull anything up. Just as well. As it was, she wasn't sure she could face seeing news about her father right now.

So she washed the dishes and placed them in the rack, then did her bedtime routine as though nothing surreal had happened since last night when she'd gotten ready for bed—washed her face, brushed her teeth, plugged her phone in to charge, then climbed into the bed and pulled up the covers. She was almost too exhausted to care if someone wanted to kill her. Too exhausted to relive the horror of the day. Or the fact that her father had died before her eyes. Grief would bury her if she let it. The fear would strangle her.

For this moment in time, she'd allow herself to believe she was safe.

Thanks to Cooper.

God, please keep him safe. Please don't let him die because he's trying to help me. And please, can this just end? Can this be the last of it?

Her mind drifted along with her body as she welcomed sleep, surprised it would come—until a noise jerked her completely awake. She sat up in bed. Moonlight spilled into the window. Hadley slipped from the bed and cracked the bedroom door open; glad she'd left the lamp on in the living room.

The back door creaked. Hadley froze.

"Hadley, it's just me." Cooper slipped inside. He glanced around the room, then caught her standing at the bedroom door.

"I'm sorry, did I wake you?"

She shut the door behind her. "It's okay. I thought you'd gone for the night or I wouldn't have locked you out."

"You were in the shower when Deputy Callahan knocked, so I thought I'd talk to him outside."

She stiffened. Mentally prepared to run. What had she been thinking to let her guard down? "Is he still here?"

"No. Relax, Hadley. He got another call. Domestic violence one town over. It'll take him an hour to get there. A search and recovery will start in the morning for the man who fell. There's nothing they can do tonight to find him. The region is too treacherous." Cooper frowned. "I've been through something similar before and that was someone I wanted to find. Someone I prayed would survive. And there was still nothing I could do."

She heard the pain in his voice, and she wanted to know that story, but he said no more about it. Deciding he might want her to change the subject, she asked, "You're sure it's a search and recovery, rather than a rescue?"

"If he's still alive, he's not waiting around for a rescue."

He'd be coming for me, then. Hadley couldn't help the shiver that ran over her.

"Don't take that wrong. What I meant is that he's dead. He's gone. It's a recovery." Cooper sagged.

"Why do I get the sense you feel guilty about what happened? Do you think you could have done something more to save him?"

"No. I tried to pull him up. And when he fell, I called for help as soon as I could. I did everything I could. He went over the edge because of me…but he was trying to kill you. It was him or you. Him or us. I don't feel guilty about that."

The way he said those last words confirmed her suspicions. He felt guilty about *something*. There was something more, something deeper bothering the man. Was it to do with someone who fell into the river that he mentioned?

As an artist, Hadley made it a habit to look beyond the obvious. To see what others couldn't. But she wouldn't push him.

"What about the deputy, Cooper? What did you tell him about me?"

"Nothing. I had just started telling him what happened when the emergency call came in and he had to leave. That'll give me the night to figure things out. He knows I fought a guy who fell in the gorge. That's enough for now."

"Oh, Cooper. Is he going to investigate to make sure you didn't murder someone today?"

"You ask too many questions. I need to go so you can get some sleep. We'll talk tomorrow."

"Are you going to call your connections?"

He shrugged. "Eventually, I guess—but not

right now. You're safe tonight, Hadley. That's all that matters. We'll figure out how to keep you safe tomorrow."

"And the next day?" Hadley wasn't sure why she prodded him. She wasn't his responsibility, after all.

Maybe she just didn't want to be alone.

She held his gaze, hating that she felt utterly exposed. Completely transparent. She could never have made a good spy, unlike her father.

Something shifted behind Cooper's steely blues. He released a sort of huff-laugh and closed the distance. What was he doing? Um…no, just no. Hadley put her hands up, prepared to defend herself.

And Cooper pulled her into his arms. Held her tight. His action surprised her. Seemed out of character, but now that she felt the comfort and strength he emanated she understood him better. He wanted to show her, in a physical way, that he could protect her. That he *would* protect her.

As if fighting off her assassin hadn't been enough.

"You've been through a lot today. But it's okay—you can rest now. Nobody's going to find you tonight. Even if they did, they'd have to go through me first."

Hadley didn't want to let go, to let herself trust,

or soak up what he was giving, but she couldn't help it. She clung to this stranger who'd risked his life for her.

What am I doing?
Cooper was usually better at controlling himself.

He'd thought by living here in Gideon surrounded by more wilderness than civilization, teaching others how to survive, he could keep the evil in this world out. But looked like it had found him all the same. He had no choice but to step up—helping Hadley was his duty. Not even his father could argue with him there.

But holding her in his arms? That wasn't exactly his duty.

He should release her, but she clung to him now, and trembled against him. Cooper didn't want to feel. Not like this. But her fear—the utter injustice of her situation—pinged against the wall around his heart. Slowly, he released her. Couldn't have imagined it would be that hard.

Holding her at arm's length, he looked into her translucent eyes, the golds and greens stunning him again. But he shook off the effect she had on him. She needed him to be a warrior, a protector, nothing more.

Both uncertainty and strength mingled behind her gaze. Good. She'd need the strength to see her through, just as he would. The uncertainty couldn't be helped.

"I don't want you to risk your life," she said. "Not for me."

Then who else would be up to the task? But Cooper didn't ask her that. "I have experience in doing just that. You should be glad you found your way here. Take comfort in that, and get some sleep."

Somehow, he needed to extract himself from this moment. She was...vulnerable. And though he never would have expected it, she'd exposed his vulnerability as well.

She nodded. "Okay...okay, I'll sleep. You get some rest, too."

Once she was at the bedroom door, she glanced back. "And, Cooper..."

"Yeah?"

"Thank you, again."

He nodded. Dead-bolted the back entrance, then he exited through the other door that opened up into the house and his business, then locked her in good and tight with his key.

He struggled to wrap his mind around the events of the day. He'd battled with a hit man—a professional assassin—and that man had warned that someone else would be sent. If he could believe the man's words, then how quickly would the next one arrive? How could he find Hadley here? There was one treacherous road into town from the coast and another from the east. That was a deterrent for some, but not for someone truly determined.

Cooper must remain vigilant.

He locked up the front door to Wilderness, Inc., and scouted the wooded area around the house. Wilderness, Inc., resided in Gideon proper, which was an unincorporated community rather than an actual town. Gideon was all about tourism, promoting the history of the town, and everything to do with the Rogue River—salmon and steelhead fishing, jet boats, white-water rapids and hiking. He walked the area around the lodges and hotels. A smoky aroma wafted through the air. Ricky's Rogue Bar-B-Q smoked meat for tomorrow's crowd, reminding him why he didn't keep anything besides eggs in his own kitchen.

No need.

He refocused on his task. A stranger could easily slip in and out, especially at the campsites scattering the woods that skirted the town. But there were no signs of anyone lurking around his business. Satisfied that Hadley was in no imminent danger, Cooper went home and locked up the storefront from the inside before settling on the couch in his small office. It wouldn't be the first time he'd slept here.

The next morning, Cooper was up before dawn and decided to let Hadley sleep in.

In the meantime, he had to prepare for the worst-case scenario. He gathered packs—everything they would need to hide in the wilderness— just in case it came to that. Deputy Callahan or someone from the county would be back this morning to talk more about the man Cooper had killed—or rather, hadn't been able to save.

He hadn't figured out what he would say about Hadley yet. He believed in justice and doing the right thing. But if telling the sheriff's department everything about her would jeopardize her life, Cooper had to be careful. He had to figure this out first, before he gave up everything he knew.

As morning light crested the mountains, he saw the town stirring through the storefront windows. Tourists and campers out early, getting ready for a day on the river or hiking the mountains. He hadn't told his family or employees the danger he'd brought with him. Hadn't even followed up with Melanie after leaving her to hike the knitting club back out.

This was all happening too fast.

That was another problem with his plan.

His business was all about strangers. People came from all over the world for an adventure excursion or wilderness training. But dealing with strangers, Wilderness, Inc., employees wouldn't know the assassin if he or she were to show. Add to that, how was Cooper going to warn them?

Melanie, who'd been engaged to his brother before he'd committed suicide, was leaving with a group today for a three-day hiking excursion. They were meeting at the trailhead and she wouldn't come here before she left. His sister, Alice, was returning from two days on the river and would be back by noon. And Gray, his younger brother, who was a special agent with the U.S. Fish and Wildlife Service, traveled a large region and might not be around for days if not weeks. Tilden was a long-time friend who'd grown up in Gideon and worked the shop when the rest of them were out. He managed the website and reservations and store purchases.

Even if he could gather them all together, how could Cooper tell any of them what to be watching for? They were experienced in many things, but knowing how to spot or fight an assassin wasn't one of them.

Cooper went to the door to unlock and open up the place. As he turned the deadlock, he glanced through the window.

A familiar sensation raked over him. Was someone watching? Had someone found Hadley already?

Cooper glanced at the dead bolt. Should he just

stay locked up today? He shook off the feeling. A dead bolt wouldn't keep the monsters away. And if someone was in town looking for Hadley, he didn't want to do anything to draw attention to him or his business.

Cooper moved back to the counter to unpack boxes of supplies while he waited on Tilden to arrive and debated calling Gray. He never got him anyway but maybe he should try. He paused to leave Gray a text. He didn't feel like getting into an argument, which was always the outcome, but he needed advice.

The sheriff or the deputy on duty would show up this morning asking more questions. And like Hadley, Cooper didn't have any answers.

Yet.

He'd give Hadley another half hour and then take breakfast upstairs, energy bars from a rack along with coffee he brewed for customers, and they could make a plan. See what was what.

Behind the counter, he pulled out his Buck knife and bent down to cut open a box on the floor. Heard the jingle over the door. He stood to greet the customer and stiffened.

A man wearing a black turtleneck and black leather jacket stood at the entrance and glanced around the shop. Something about him seemed off. Maybe it was the way he scanned the room, as though doing reconnaissance. Instinct kicked in, telling Cooper this man was dangerous. Was he here for Hadley?

"Can I help you?"

The man turned around and locked the door behind him.

SIX

Cooper didn't wait for an answer.

Ducking behind the counter, he grabbed the Judge, his Remington 870 Express double-barrel shotgun—the greatest home-defense firearm ever created, if you asked him. He could stop this guy in his tracks and not worry about bullets penetrating the walls and killing anyone on the street. The Judge only cared about bringing justice, not harming innocent bystanders.

"You answered my question before I even asked." The man's voice sounded crisp. Focused. "She's here."

Cooper pumped the shotgun. "What do you want with her?"

"Looks like you already know. If you don't want anyone else you care about to be harmed, come out and we can finish this without any collateral damage."

"I don't think so." Cooper crawled quietly to the end of the counter.

"I thought you might say that."

Gunfire resounded, the noise barely contained by a suppressor. Bullets ripped into the wooden counter, some hitting the boxes.

Time for you to meet the Judge.

Cooper fired the shotgun, then crawled behind gear, clothes and equipment, hoping Hadley wouldn't come down to investigate.

The shot didn't hit his target, but apparently it was enough to start him griping. "Putting you both down quickly is too good for you. You made me come out here into the middle of no-man's-land, only reachable by a ridiculous scenic route behind slow people who don't know how to drive. I wouldn't have signed on if I had known."

Just keep talking. Give me something I can use. He had to guard the office and access to the staircase to his apartment. Cooper pumped the shotgun again.

"Who sent you?"

In reply gunfire from the assassin's semiautomatic weapon riddled the shop.

Did the assassin think he wouldn't draw attention from outside with that suppressor? Gunfire still echoed loudly. Cooper hadn't wanted the sheriff to show up but he quickly changed his mind.

Now would be a good time, Sheriff Kruse. I could use the backup.

Crawling forward, he found a place to position himself and fired off his own weapon, aiming straight and true, necessary when firing at close ranges even with a shotgun, but the guy took cover.

Had he hit him?

"The law is already on their way. I'm expecting the sheriff any minute."

Nothing. He would have expected a mocking laugh from the jerk, at least.

By now, Hadley had to have stirred. He glanced up and saw the bullet holes in the ceiling.

Get out, Hadley. Go, now!

If she snuck out through the back entrance, she might be able to escape. Somehow Cooper would find her. But that was the problem wasn't it? If Cooper could find her, so could this assassin. Cooper moved from behind the boxes of wilderness survival kits. Then over to the rack of Igloo sleeping bags. The store didn't carry much but about now he wished for much more stock.

Sweat beaded his brow.

This was life and death.

Images of the Middle East accosted him. He was sure he'd battled this guy before, metaphorically speaking.

His breaths came too quickly. Too loudly.

Breathe in... Breathe...out.

From here, he could see his office door. He

didn't think the assassin was in there, but he couldn't be sure. If he shot off another volley, he'd give his position away.

God, help me. Where is this man? Help me take him out.

Like taking the last guy out had worked so well. Why would anyone go to so much trouble to kill Hadley? Unless there was something she wasn't telling him.

Okay. His office was directly in front of him. From there he could access the stairs and the apartment. If Hadley was still there, they could escape out the back.

He measured his breaths, working up the nerve to make a mad dash.

There were only two places the man could be hiding. Crouching, Cooper inched forward, then stood slowly so he could see, fire off his shotgun again, then run for it.

Arms wrapped around his neck. The muzzle of a gun pierced his side. Cooper twisted at the same instant a bullet ripped through, only grazing Cooper, before catching empty space and hitting the wall.

Cooper found himself in hand-to-hand combat. Again.

Pain lashed his stomach, his sides, his kidneys, as the man beat him, slipping through Cooper's attempts to shield his body while defending himself from Cooper's offensive moves. Bullets shredded boxes of equipment as Cooper turned aside the firearm aimed at him, again and again. Supplies tumbled. Shredded sleeping bags and racks toppled.

And somewhere behind him a woman screamed.

His mind flashed back to the scream in the wilderness.

Hadley!

She was screaming. She was here now.

"Get out! Go, why are you still here?" he tried to tell her, but all that came out of his mouth were grunts as he fought what he knew was a death battle.

This time there wasn't a cliff for this guy to fall from. The assassin's dark eyes slivered, then telegraphed there was something behind Cooper. Or someone.

Hadley. He would go for Hadley. The man lunged away from Cooper and went for the Judge splayed on the floor where Cooper had lost it during the fight. Cooper charged after him.

Click, click.

The shotgun fired off right over his head a millisecond before Cooper rammed into the man and drove his fist into the attacker's gut.

Hadley screamed again.

God, help me!

Then Cooper was on top of the man, his hands

around his throat. Squeezing. Tighter. Harder. Forcing the life from him.

Hadley's voice resounded in his ear.

"What are you doing? Don't kill him!"

Alive.

She was still alive.

And he eased back. A mistake. The assassin beneath him took advantage of the opening and pressed his thumbs into Cooper's eye. Fire burned his eyes but he broke away before it was too late, falling backward and away from the man.

"Run, Hadley!" He choked out the words on her approach.

But she engaged the new man sent to kill her, with those Krav Maga skills he'd seen before. Cooper caught his breath. He didn't want to see her get into this again. Had wanted to protect her. He dove at the assassin, disengaging him from Hadley, and received a punch to the temple.

Darkness edged his vision.

Cooper!

In her peripheral vision, Hadley could see him stagger, then drop. Was he dead?

Someone else killed because of her?

An ache pinged inside as the thought registered in the back of her mind while she continued to fight. She'd practiced so much with her father and he'd insisted that she keep up her practice even when he was gone, so her moves were simple reflex.

Cross body punch.

Elbow strike.

Counter the assassin's front kick.

A small space for a kick, and he had her in defensive mode, moving her back into a corner.

Then he went for her throat, just like the other one had. Her reflexes fell away—she wasn't used to sparring against someone who was actually aiming to kill. This wasn't who Hadley was. She wasn't a fighter. Not like this. Could she even survive? Too late, she realized she'd let fear crawl under her skin and paralyze her. Rake away her reflexive actions.

This man, this…this assassin wanted to look in her eyes and watch her die as he strangled her. Without another thought or defensive move, Hadley ducked and slipped away behind a pile of clothes on a toppled rack. Her father hadn't taught her to give up, or to run, but that's exactly what she was doing now.

Whimpers sprang from her of their own volition. She threw boxes and heaved a display case at him. Anything to keep him from getting to her.

"Why are you trying to kill me? I don't even know you! I saved your life moments ago, when I asked him not to kill you!" She'd been an idiot, then.

He grinned, a sick, twisted grin. His eyes were stone-cold. Dead.

"On second thought, the travel to this place on the map was well worth it. I haven't been given such a worthy fight in ages, if ever. I haven't seen such a spitfire or this kind of determination in spite of the fear I see in your eyes. If only I could keep you alive for a little longer, just to play with you."

He pointed the weapon at her.

Time stood still. She gazed at the muzzle of the weapon he held. Seconds ticked by in her head, seeming to last for hours.

Is this it?

Am I going to die now, Lord?

It seemed so unfair. Life was too short. How could she right the wrong of her father's death?

But something moved. In a flash, Cooper rammed into the gunman. The weapon fired off.

Hadley fell in the wall behind her. The world went black.

The whole shelf stocked with books, tactical gear and tents collapsed on top of the assassin, giving Cooper time to grab hold of the Judge. Appreciating the weapon in his hands once again, he scrambled from beneath the chaos and stood to his feet.

Pumped the shotgun.

Click, click...

Fired the weapon into the shop as the assassin darted behind a wall. Then, to Cooper's surprise, he crashed out the front window of Wilderness, Inc.

Cooper jumped up and ran after him, but couldn't spot him. Just like that, the man had disappeared.

Two fiftyish men standing on the porch of the lodge across the way stared, wide-eyed. A family climbing from their minivan looked on, as well. Had they heard the chaos? Apparently so. Then why hadn't anyone thought to help? But maybe it had all happened so quickly. It was just as well. Anyone getting in the assassin's way would have been killed.

Cooper needed to chase the man down. There was only an entire wilderness in which he could hide.

But Hadley...

"Hadley." Her name came out in a huff.

He jumped through the window and made a beeline for where he'd seen her go down. Had she been shot? A pang ran through Cooper's chest. *Hadley.*

He searched through the mess that used to be his wilderness survival store.

God, where is she? Please let her be okay.

There. She was on the floor beneath the vests.

Cooper shoved them out of the way and off Hadley's body. He had too much stuff in this store, after all. When had it gotten so filled with all this junk?

Lifting her into his arms, he felt for a pulse in her neck and found one. His own heart started up again. Then he searched for an injury. A gunshot wound. Bleeding.

But nothing. He found nothing.

Why was she unconscious? Had she hit her head?

He pressed his hand against her cheek, feeling her soft skin. "Hadley, wake up."

Come on, come on. He frowned. Was she going to be all right? He assessed her injuries again. All he saw were bruises and scratches from her wilderness battle with the enemy yesterday and this morning.

She groaned. Her lids fluttered. Then her eyes locked with his—this time looking like emeralds in spun gold. She sucked in a breath and sat up. "What...what happened?" Hadley looked around. "Where is he?"

"Gone."

"For now? Or forever?"

"I wish it was forever but I have a feeling he'll be back."

"Why did he leave?"

Frowning, Cooper shook his head. "I don't know. Maybe the Judge got him."

"The Judge?"

"My home and business defense system." Cooper lifted the shotgun.

"Oh. I hope you got him good."

"Not good enough or he wouldn't have been able to leave. But at least I scared him off for now."

"He was only playing. Making us pay for the trouble to find me."

Cooper nodded. "No more games."

She sighed, but nodded her agreement. "It's shoot for keeps next time."

Cooper would prefer the games, but she was right. Next time, they might not get any warning.

"How's your head?"

She scrunched up her face. "It's not bad. I honestly… I don't know what happened. One second I was staring down the barrel of a gun. I thought… I thought he would finally kill me." Her voice hitched at those last words.

Could she have fainted? But it didn't matter. "We need to get out of here."

He assisted her up.

She looked around, horror morphing her features. "Oh, Cooper. Your store! I'm so, so sorry."

He followed her gaze. Yeah. What a mess.

"You're alive. I'm alive. That's all what matters. Wouldn't you agree?"

She shrugged, her strawberry-blond curls askew from the morning's battle. "Hard not to."

A few faces peeked in through the shattered front window. Some tried the door. "Cooper? You okay in there?"

"Give us a minute!" he called, then to Hadley, he said, "Why did you come downstairs? Why did you try to get in the middle of the fight? You could have been killed." He released her. Backed away. He kicked an Igloo sleeping bag. "What's the point in trying to protect you if you're going to expose yourself like that?" He couldn't help the anger…it erupted from some deep and painful place inside that he'd tried to forget about. It was actually aimed at himself for failing her—failing his brother—but it deflected on her.

And he hated himself for it. Squeezed his eyes shut. Blew out a breath, then sucked in another. "Look, Hadley, I shouldn't have said that. I'm… sorry."

He risked a glance at her and wished he hadn't. The look in her eyes—the pain and shock of it. He'd driven home his point all right.

He hadn't expected for the look in her eyes to stab right through him. What was it about Hadley Mason that negated the years of experience he had in protecting himself? He shouldn't care so much that his words had been harsh and had hurt her. He couldn't hope to help her if his emotions clouded the way.

And maybe, not even then.

She frowned. "It's okay. I deserved it. You're right, of course. I shouldn't have come down. But I heard the gunfire. I wanted to make sure you were okay. I couldn't just let you fight him alone—not when he was here for *me*, not you. Do you understand? This was my problem, and now you've inserted yourself into things, for which I'm grateful. I know I couldn't have survived this long without help. But I hate that you're risking yourself like this."

Cooper hung his head, unsure what else there was to say.

"I'll help you clean up here. I need to run upstairs. Change into something besides sweats."

"Don't worry about cleaning up. Gather your stuff, what little you brought."

"Why?"

"We're getting out of here."

"We're not going to stay?"

"No. Hurry, now."

She nodded and ran up the steps to his apartment. He listened to the door open and shut.

Ramming his hands through his hair, he paced, kicking the mess around. He was at a crossroads. He'd worked so hard to order his life. Live in a place where life was a simple matter of man versus nature. And *that*, he could handle. He was out of his depth in this situation.

Maybe he wasn't the right person to help her, after all. He'd failed her, keeping her here so the assassin could find her. She needed someone more than Cooper. Deep down, he knew that.

He'd been a disappointment to his father. He hadn't been able to save his brother. And he definitely wasn't enough for Hadley.

But he was the only one here at the moment. The only one who was remotely qualified. The job was his, whether he wanted it or not. He'd give everything he had to protect her and that meant he couldn't focus on his past failures if he hoped to keep her alive. Keep *them* alive, since her survival depended on his survival. At the very least, he knew what to do now. He had to draw this madman away from Gideon and somehow protect Hadley at the same time.

SEVEN

Gasping for breath, Hadley leaned against the door.

That had been close, so close. Again!

She'd been found again.

And by a different guy. Was he working with the last one? At the very least, the man who'd put out a contract on her knew her whereabouts. And he seemed to have a team of killers at his disposal.

Who was he? If only her father could have told her more. Told her something she could use in this battle to stay alive.

Anger boiled beneath the surface, ready to erupt. Whoever this man was behind the contract, he'd killed her father. That should be enough to make her crazy for revenge. But she was running for her life instead. She didn't like having to look over her shoulder. Having to fear that at any moment she could be attacked. She didn't want to run and hide, she wanted to stay and fight.

But God help her, she'd fled in fear during her fight with the assassin in Cooper's store.

She lived her life with purpose—with goals and dreams—and some stranger had taken everything from her when he'd killed her father and now sought to kill her, twisting everything around until her only purpose was to live another day.

Hadley had to find a way to twist things back.

Cooper had sent her up to her room to grab her things. Pack her bag. Oh, she was packing all right. She had the clothes on her back and just one other set of jeans and T-shirt, hoodie and jacket. That was as far as she'd gotten. And he was right about one thing, wrong about another.

She wasn't staying here. But they weren't leaving together.

Cooper didn't know it yet, but she was going it alone. After changing into jeans, sticking her hair in a rubber band and tugging on her cap, she stuffed her toiletries and sweats in the pack she'd bought.

She dropped the bag to the rumpled bed and shoved her hair back from her eyes. She didn't want to leave him behind, but she couldn't think of anything else to do.

They were both scared.

That much had been clear from his outburst. The look in his eyes.

And it terrified her to think that Cooper Wilde had been scared—for his life and for hers. She was nothing but trouble for him.

She could not be the reason another person died. The list was already far too long. She tugged on her backpack full of cash and her fake passport, grabbed her bag of meager belongings and slipped out the door for the back steps and hurried to the clunker. Fortunately, Cooper had left the keys on the coffee table, trusting her to stay put.

Though she wasn't sure where she was going, she knew she needed to find another place in the wilderness to hide out. Maybe she could use the survival tips pamphlet she'd grabbed from the toppled display and actually survive. Disappear long enough to be forgotten or assumed dead.

I'll get a guard dog. Call him Benji. No, that sounds too friendly. What about Jaws?

She'd train him to attack anything with two legs that moved and wasn't her. Hadley would become a hermit until a year or maybe ten down the road, when the contract on her life would fall off.

If it ever did.

Was ten years long enough?

She'd seen enough violence, enough brutality, to last a lifetime. But it was better to be alone than to involve Cooper more than he already was. His store had already been destroyed because of her.

She wouldn't stay here so that anything else was destroyed, or others were hurt.

This was it, then. She was leaving the one person who could help her. Hadley leaned forward, pressing her forehead into the steering wheel.

Was she ready to go it alone? She'd been running for her life when she'd first arrived here, and hadn't had a chance to think about how utterly alone she really was, especially since her father was dead. He'd been such a lifeline for her. Cheering her on, encouraging her toward her dreams.

And for what?

Tears surged. Hadley lifted her head and swiped them away. She had to trust her father had given her all the tools she would need to survive. And they would have to be enough.

Remembering the trouble she'd had starting the clunker yesterday, she jabbed the keys in and sent up a silent prayer. *Please, God, please God, please, God...let it start.*

"And please, don't let him notice until I'm long gone."

The Jeep's engine turned over, making entirely too much noise.

Now, how did she get out of here without being seen? Cooper was one thing, but what about the man who'd come to kill her? He was still out there.

Somewhere.

* * *

Cooper had texted his brother, Special Agent Grayson Wilde, but he hadn't actually expected to see him in the flesh and at the worst possible moment, stepping into the shop by way of the shattered window.

Gray crunched across the broken glass, his stern gaze taking in the chaotic scene.

"I didn't expect to see you this soon," Cooper admitted. Nor was he sure he was glad to see his brother.

He'd contacted him, yes. He needed someone to know what was going on and maybe Gray had a few ideas of what to do, but on the other hand, every conversation between the two of them was a battle. He and Gray never saw eye-to-eye on anything. They loved each other like brothers should. But agree on anything? Nope.

Gray shook his head, incredulous. "What happened? Want to tell me what's going on?"

"I don't have a lot of time, so I'll tell you what I can." Cooper glanced up to the ceiling, hoping Hadley would understand him sharing her story. He knew she wouldn't like it, but this was his brother. Yeah, he worked for a law enforcement entity, but Cooper could trust him the truth and with their lives.

So he spilled everything. "And right now, I'm

gathering everything I can to make a run for the wilderness and survive. Never thought I'd actually have to use the skills, at least like this."

"That's quite a story." Gray started helping Cooper stuff prepackaged survival kits into a couple of big backpacks.

"So what do you think? What else can I do?" Cooper asked.

"You have to find out who's behind this," Gray said. "You know the number to call. Have you done that?"

Cooper frowned. Was he that desperate yet?

Gray eyed Cooper. "Don't let pride get you and this girl killed."

"Pride's got nothing to do with it."

"Maybe I should make that call, if you won't."

And the battle begins. Had Cooper expected anything less than an argument with Gray? But he didn't have time for this. "I only contacted you so someone would know where I'd gone, and what I'm doing. See if you had some thoughts."

"And I shared those."

Cooper stopped packing and stood tall to face his brother. "I'll make the call if it comes to that. This isn't your burden to bear. It's mine."

Gray shook his head, disappointment clear in his gaze. "Jeremy said the same thing to you, how many times?"

"Nice of you to bring that up. I wasn't able to help him. So your point is moot."

"You called me. Brought me in on this. What I'm saying is that the guilt you feel from failing him is always in your eyes, Cooper. I don't want that to worsen if something happens to this girl because you wouldn't make the phone call. You wanted my advice. I'm giving it."

"Honestly, I haven't had time to think it through. To process everything. It all happened so fast, and this guy, the one who brought a contract on her, I have a feeling that he's relentless, just like his assassins."

"So you will make the call then?"

Cooper didn't want to think about it. Maybe he could handle it on his own. He'd prefer it that way. "If it comes to that."

"Will you listen to yourself? You're putting your life and this girl's life at risk for no reason."

"Have a little faith in me, will you?"

Satisfied the packs were ready, Cooper dropped them and mentally checked off half of what he'd really like to take on this covert expedition. Water bottles, flashlights, multi-tools, knives, MREs, first-aid kit, compass. He needed more than he'd packed, but there was no time.

And besides, didn't he teach people how to survive in the wilderness without anything at all?

Gray studied him, and Copper knew his brother was waiting for him to come to his senses.

He gave a subtle shake of his head. He wasn't going to change his mind. Gray didn't expect him to agree, anyway.

"I'm going to disappear with her until this is over. Until we figure out what to do next."

"Is there anything else you need me to do?"

"Yeah. You're part owner of the business. You have a share in it. Let everyone know to meet their clients anywhere but here. And maybe you can clean this up while you're at it." Cooper just had to throw that in, but he seasoned it with a teasing smirk.

His features hard, Gray scowled.

"I have to get out of here," Cooper continued. "So at least board up the window for me before you head out."

"Cooper…" Gray shifted his feet, clearly disturbed. "I don't like this at all. Please, be careful. I'll see what I can find out through my channels."

His brother's reaction hit Cooper in the gut. Gray didn't usually show his hand, reveal his concern so outwardly. Noting that the situation disturbed his brother, Cooper felt his own doubts ramping up. Was he the guy for this task? But he wouldn't let Gray see his misgivings.

"Find out what you can. As long as you don't

give Hadley away, make yourself a target or give away my locations or plans, I'm good with that."

Gray nodded.

"I need to get Hadley and get out of here before someone comes back." Before it was too late. He had the feeling he'd had already wasted too much time.

He climbed the steps and knocked on the door. No answer. No shuffling inside. Nothing. Oh, no. His gut clenched. Had the assassin found and killed her while Cooper wasted time downstairs?

Cooper opened the door, burst through the apartment. "Hadley?"

Quiet answered him. He searched the small space. Her things were gone. He ran down the stairs at the back and the Jeep was gone, too. He sprinted around the house to the main street through town.

He caught a flash of the back of the Jeep as it disappeared down the road headed east. Gray's vehicle sat in front of the store. Cooper hopped in, grateful the keys were in the ignition like he'd expected. Gray would understand.

Cooper backed the vehicle away from Wilderness, Inc., and just before he floored it, Gray jumped in the passenger side.

"What do you think you're doing?" Gray strapped himself in.

"Smart you jumped in."

"I knew you wouldn't stop for me."

"It's Hadley. She's leaving without me."

"This could be your chance, Cooper, to leave well enough alone."

"Right. Like you would leave her if she'd fallen in your lap."

He pressed his foot on the accelerator to speed up until he was right up on the Jeep's rear. He'd caught up with her, sure, but he'd have to make her stop and think. Cooper honked, laying on the horn. He could see her eyes, shaded by the cap, in the rearview mirror. They stared back at him, loaded with sadness and frustration. He motioned for her to pull over but she kept going.

Cooper sounded the horn again and kept on honking. She had to know he wasn't going to let her go. Hadley swerved to the right of the narrow mountain road and stopped. Cooper was out and at her door before she had a chance to change her mind.

"Where do you think you're going?"

"I need to get some place safe. I don't want to involve you."

"I'm already involved. I've fought an assassin on your behalf twice now. I'm probably a target, too—with or without you."

Gray marched up behind him.

Hadley eyed Gray, her accusing tone meant for Cooper. "You told him?"

"There's nobody I trust more than my brother." Except maybe Alice, his sister, but he didn't need to bring that up now. Nor did he want Alice to be caught in the cross fire.

Stepping out of the Jeep, she put her hands on her hips. "And now there's yet another person who could get killed because of me."

"Hadley Mason, meet Gray Wilde." Cooper left off the special agent part.

"You can trust Coop to protect you," Gray said. "He knows what he's doing and will keep you safe until we get to the bottom of this."

"Our attacker could be out there, aiming for our heads even now, Hadley. Let's go back and finish gearing up. I packed for a long stay, and then we'll get lost where nobody can find us."

"But what about your business?"

"Wilderness, Inc., can survive without me. Gray's going to make sure the staff regroups and meets their clients at other locations. The business doesn't depend on the store. It's all taken care of. So, what do you say?" Cooper held his breath. Couldn't remember the last time anxiety had clung to him like this as he waited for her answer.

Indecision emanated from Hadley's golden

green gaze. She searched the thick woods surrounding them.

"This is life or death, Hadley," he said. "The decision you make now could mean the difference in saving your life."

"And causing your death," she added.

A twig snapped and echoed through the silence. They instinctively ducked. Was someone out there watching, listening?

"You guys go on, I'll check it out," Gray offered. "Probably an animal."

"Gray...wait." Cooper hesitated, second-guessing his decision to bring his brother into this. Seeing the determination in Gray's face, though, he let it go. "Be careful."

"This is what I do, remember?"

"Not sure you've faced this kind of criminal element before."

"If he was that good, you'd already be dead." Gray scowled. "Now would you get her out of here?"

"Come on. Let's go." Cooper ushered her around to the passenger seat of the Jeep, like she'd already agreed to go back with him.

You'd already be dead...

Then why weren't they? He knew the two guys he'd fought were professional grade. Cooper was good, but he wasn't of that caliber. It had to be the simple fact they were out of their element, here in the wilderness. And that was an advantage Cooper had every intention of using.

It was a matter of life or death.

EIGHT

What am I doing? Did it even make sense that half an hour ago she was on her way out of town without Cooper Wilde? Her attempt at cutting him loose had been feeble at best.

Back at the house, he loaded up his more-than-adequate GMC Yukon with gear to survive in the wilderness for a year. Well, maybe not that long, but it looked like it to Hadley.

When it was time to leave, he insisted on her driving. She maneuvered his big, honking gully-crossing, mud-trudging SUV around the curvy mountain lane that hugged a rocky wall on one side, hedged close to a river-worn crack in the earth on the other.

Hadley's focus was on the road and nothing else. Maybe that had been his plan or maybe he didn't realize how nervous she was on this crazy path.

"So, what happened to our latest attacker? Why do you think he just disappeared? Do you really think you shot him?" She'd been wondering about that. Why would he just give up and run out of the store otherwise?

"He must be injured. I shot off the Judge into the store, not taking any particular aim, just before he crashed through the window to escape."

"Do you think he's too injured to recover?"

"He was strong enough to barrel through that window and get away from me when I gave chase, so I don't think the injury's fatal. As long as he can get treatment or treat himself in time, he'll survive. That said, my guess is that he went somewhere to regroup."

"You're sure he's coming back for me, then."

Cooper shifted in the seat. "I think we have to be prepared. That's why we're going into hiding. Somewhere he can't find you."

"But for how long?"

"As long as it takes."

He said nothing more but she could tell his thoughts were on hyperdrive like hers were.

Then, finally, he said, "Someone is going to a lot of trouble here, Hadley. You sure you've told me everything?"

"You think I would hold anything back from you?"

When he hesitated, she glanced over at him, then back to the road, more than a little hurt. Anger boiled up.

He sighed. "Not intentionally. But maybe there's something you haven't thought of."

She forced herself to take a deep breath and reply calmly. "Okay, that makes sense. I'll keep thinking but as far as I know, I have told you everything that happened."

"Try thinking back on your relationship with your father. His friends, his travels, anything at all that might clue you in."

"Cooper, do you hear yourself? You're reaching here. My father only mentioned that it might be connected to a past operation. He wasn't specific. Maybe he didn't even know what this was about."

Oh, God, how am I ever going to survive this... this spy thing, the CIA with its assassins? This isn't my world. How can I fight a horde of killers? She'd lost her mother and father, questioned everything her father had ever told her, and right now, she wasn't even sure God was listening.

Never had she felt so forsaken.

Tears burned behind her eyes, but she blinked them away. Swallowed the knot in her throat.

Except for Cooper, she would be entirely alone in this.

Thanks, God. Maybe...maybe You do see and You do hear what I'm going through. Maybe You sent Cooper to help me.

She felt the man's eyes on her, but didn't look

at him. He was…attractive. She couldn't deny that, which made this whole situation worse. She didn't want to be drawn to him, to care about him. People she cared about died, and Cooper was certainly in a position to take a bullet for her. Could she really spend an indefinite period of time alone with him attempting to survive in the wilderness? It seemed surreal to even consider it.

Except her father's death and everything that had followed were equally surreal.

"Okay, slow down here and turn off onto that road."

"Seriously?"

A big red warning sign had been nailed to a tree.

Hadley read the sign out loud just in case Cooper couldn't read. "Danger. Remote Road System Ahead. Danger. You could get stranded and die."

"That's meant for strangers who don't know their way around. A couple of years back a family got stranded."

"And died?"

"Only one of them."

"You're a real confidence builder, Cooper Wilde."

"I do my best."

Hadley steered the vehicle onto the road and gently inched forward. The Yukon rocked but handled the gravelly road. "So, why even have a road if you're going to post a sign?"

"The sign's meant to discourage cars—logging trucks run this road all the time."

"Are we going to run into one of those coming from the other direction?"

"I can't make any guarantees."

A boulder loomed ahead, blocking at least half the road. Hadley jerked on the wheel a little too much for comfort, given the narrowness of the road and the ridge to her left.

"Easy now, just slow down. You're doing fine." His voice had that smooth, reassuring tone, but he didn't sound convinced himself.

She came to a complete stop, though she could have driven around the boulder. Hadley leaned forward to peer out the windshield and upward as much as possible. "Boulders just come crashing down like that? How often does that happen?"

"It's just one of those things Hadley... When..." His words trailed off.

Right. Just one of those things. "When it's your time to go, it's your time to go. Is that the rest of what you were going to say?"

"I wasn't going to say anything. Try not to be so fatalistic. Don't focus on the potential for a boulder dropping from the sky around every corner."

"Or an assassin stepping into the middle of the road and firing at me point-blank."

"Not likely. We're seriously off grid here. This road isn't even maintained. In the winter, we couldn't hope to go this way. Too much snow."

After her first attempt to hide had been thwarted, Hadley hadn't been sure simply going off grid in the wilderness would be enough. But she had been trying to go underground on her own. Maybe Cooper was the missing ingredient. He knew the area very well, and was more capable than she was of going deep into parts unknown. As a matter of fact, she couldn't even survive more than a few miles away from a town.

She risked a glance at him. He hadn't cleaned up after his fight with the assassin. Did she look as rough as he did? Probably, but she was sure she didn't look as good. He was pure, rugged masculinity.

Was she crazy to run off with this stranger? Maybe, but she'd have been crazier not to.

Considering her world had now turned upside down, she couldn't afford to turn down a stranger's help. Maybe she should try to remedy that. To somehow move beyond stranger status.

She turned her attention back to steering around the boulder, careful when the Yukon came close to the edge. "You sure you don't want to do this?"

"You're doing such a great job, why would I?"

Oh, he was so funny. "Listen, I want to apologize for running off on you."

"That's okay," he said. "It's understandable."

"Is it? Seems kind of lame, but I can't stand the thought of someone else getting hurt because of me. I'm not sure that going into the wilderness with you right now is the best decision. But I don't know what else to do."

"I'll do everything in my power to make sure we both survive this. I can't help but think that our paths collided for a reason."

"You mean God put us together?"

"I don't believe in coincidence."

"Are you actually saying that someone killed my father, and then I got on that plane to Medford and rented a cabin just so it would put me in your path while you were leading a group of hikers?"

"I don't pretend to understand how God works, or the makings of the universe. How it happened doesn't matter, anymore. The point is you're here now. We're in this together."

Hadley was still trying to figure out how she felt about that. She doubted she'd be able to reconcile the chaos of her confusing emotions anytime soon. The road grew more hazardous and she had to take it even slower. After she'd been driving several hours, she would have thought they'd traveled a decent distance, but maybe they'd only gone thirty miles, if that.

She wanted a break. "Are you sure you don't want to drive?"

"I'm sure I'll get my chance."

"Where are we going anyway?" She couldn't believe she hadn't asked earlier. Getting safely out of Gideon had distracted her.

"As you've already discovered, there are only two ways in and out of town if you take the conventional methods. We're headed toward the coast, but we've veered off the main road. We're going to veer off this road, too, and at some point hike in deep." He sounded excited by the prospect.

"What about your vehicle? Won't someone find that?"

"I have a plan. You still don't trust me?"

That was the billion-dollar question. "It's hard for me to answer that. Remember, I just found out my father lied to me my entire life." She had to question everything she'd ever been told, even all the stories about her mother. "I get why he lied, and I don't blame him. Or at least, I'm trying not to. But now, I'm paying the price for his career choice. He…" Grief clogged her throat. "He paid the price, too."

"It takes some kind of trust for you to let me help you. I know that."

She couldn't let her emotions get the best of

her while she was driving. Had to focus on the road. Time enough to process everything later.

"What are the dilapidated structures I've seen out here, anyway? Cabins, too. Does anyone live in them?"

"Claims. What you're seeing are old mining claims—the flumes, stamp mills. Trestles."

"As in gold?"

"Yep. There are hundreds of them. Most we've seen predate the wilderness designation, just like some of the private property where you see a house here and there."

"So are they still active? As in are people still trying to pan for gold or mine it?"

"Some are. There are even new claims being staked. One president will get into office and withdraw thousands of acres from any new claims, only to have that reversed by the next president. I wish people would leave well enough alone—prospecting can be toxic to the rivers and the wildlife. But let's not talk politics. Turn in here."

Hadley slowed the vehicle. She didn't see anything. "Where?"

"Just...there!"

She slammed on the brakes. "I didn't see a place to turn."

Cooper's laugh came from some place deep. She'd never heard anything like it. Hadley could get used to that laugh. A good thing, too, since it looked like they were going to be spending some serious time together.

She shifted into Reverse and slowly backed up. "I...don't see a thing."

"Hold on." Cooper climbed out of the vehicle and left the road, pushing some brush out of the way.

"Oh, there is it." Hadley steered off the road and into what barely passed for a trail, the Yukon bumping and pitching, and then she stopped, just as the brush fell back in place and covered the entrance to the road again.

Did he expect her to get out? There wasn't actually anywhere to walk. Small trees and bushes filled the space between the larger trees.

Cooper climbed back in on the passenger side and looked at her. "You good to keep driving?"

Hadley stared ahead. "Wha—? I...no. I can't tell where I'm going."

He grinned. "I'm only teasing. This is one of the largest wilderness areas left. Unprotected and roadless, sort of. But those of us who live here, we know where to find a few roads, though they're mostly part of the old trail systems now. We're going to hike through to a nearby waterfall and take a break."

"What? I have a killer after me. Did you forget?"

"He won't find us here. We've been driving for hours."

"Maybe we have, but I don't think we've gone far."

He chuckled. "There's more to go and then some hiking." He reached into the backseat and pulled out a big paper bag filled with barbecue he'd picked up from the place next door before they'd headed out of Gideon.

The aroma had been taunting her for hours.

"I thought we could eat dinner here."

"Oh, well, in that case." Hadley's stomach rumbled. Had they really been driving since morning? "Let me carry the sack."

Hadley reached for it at the same time as Cooper. They grabbed hands along with the sack. Hadley would have pulled her hand away, but Cooper didn't let go. He held her captive. Who was this stranger who was risking everything for her? It didn't make sense. What kind of person would do that? She had the feeling that Cooper Wilde wasn't like anyone she'd ever met or ever would meet.

If trusting her father, a man she knew and adored, had brought her here, where would trusting a stranger like Cooper Wilde lead her?

He was three parts crazy, leading a woman he'd only met yesterday to this waterfall—one

of his favorite places, though seriously out of the
way. And that was the beauty of it—the falls remained mostly undisturbed by humans. Hardly
anyone would think to look for them here. As
it turned out, this stop was a halfway point and
they both needed a break from the rigors of the
mountain road.

With a long night ahead of them, they needed
to refuel, stretch their legs and rest.

He led the way to the waterfall, pushing past
the thick ferns, around Douglas firs and past the
orange, peeling bark of madrone trees, guiding
Hadley until he came down to the bottom of a
horseshoe ridge. Water flowed from a narrow
place at the top, then hit the ridge again where it
cascaded. Thick green moss covered everything
surrounding the falls, including boulders, logs
and the base of trees.

Cooper waited for her gasp and wasn't disappointed. Her reaction to the grandeur around
them made him smile.

Breathing in the fresh air, he settled on a log
and soaked up the soothing sounds of nature. For
the moment, they were safe.

"It's beautiful here, Coop. Uh…can I call you
Coop? I heard your brother call you that. I kind
of like it."

He found a flat boulder they could share. "Do
you, now?"

"I do." Though tired from the drive and the stress of having a killer after her, Hadley smiled.

Cooper honestly wouldn't have thought she had it in her. She surprised him. He didn't know too many people who were as resilient, and he was especially attuned to testing endurance in wilderness training. People often gave up long before they should, and dealing with that was part of his training—teaching people to dig down deep to a place they didn't even know existed inside them, find the grit and survive. He wasn't sure he could teach Hadley more than what she was learning in this real-life survival scenario. She had already found the strength to survive.

She had what it took, and now it was a simple matter of completing her survival toolbox. Krav Maga was in that toolkit, but that skill wouldn't help her stay safe and warm, out of the elements, or provide her with clean water or food. Those were things Cooper could teach her even as he was protecting her from a killer. He might as well put his time with her to good use.

Hadley propped herself on the rock and opened the sack. "Smells fantastic."

"Why do you think I built my business right next door?"

Hadley laughed softly. The sound was a pleasant addition to the waterfall and melted naturally into their surroundings. She pulled out two wrapped sandwiches and handed one over to him. "Barbecue sandwiches?"

"Sloppy joes." He grabbed it, anxious to eat. He took the can of soda she offered as well.

He had MREs and other supplies in the packs. And of course, they could eat right from the land, if they had to. But that would be the worst-case scenario and only if he couldn't eat Ricky's Rogue Bar-B-Q.

Foliage across the pool shifted. Cooper pressed his hand against his weapon hidden beneath his jacket. A deer peeked through, then disappeared, obviously disappointed two humans were taking up space at the watering hole. Relief swooshed through Cooper, though he knew it wouldn't be long-lived. He didn't know how the assassin had found her to begin with.

But find her now. I dare you.

He kept those thoughts to himself. Hubris could be a dangerous thing in this situation. In most cases, his wilderness survival training was meant for those who backpacked and hiked on their own and just wanted basic skills in case they got lost and needed to last until someone found them.

But this…getting lost on purpose…was something he'd only ever considered in the darkest recesses of his mind. Now he had an excuse to do it, but this wasn't about Cooper's secret need to hide away from his failures. This was about Hadley.

She finished off her sandwich and sighed. "When this is over, I don't suppose I could convince you to bring me back here one day so I could paint this amazing scenery."

Paint it? Oh yeah, the artist thing. Why couldn't Jeremy have found solace in painting here?

With the lush forest and moss backdrop, the green in her eyes appeared almost luminous. It was a struggle to pull his gaze away. He admired the strength and endurance he'd seen in her so far, but that was as far as he could let it go. Simple admiration. He wasn't sure how long he would need to stay hidden in the wilderness with her. How long could he fight his attraction?

"It's a deal." Cooper grabbed their trash and stuck it back into the sack. "Tell me about your painting. You mentioned something about a national debut."

Observing the falls, she lifted her chin, revealing her long slender neck. "Yes. In Portland. I have a degree in fine arts and my paintings have been featured in local and regional exhibitions, but this was supposed to be my chance to really start to make a name for myself. It takes time, usually years, to climb the ladder."

"Interesting. Art is like the business world in that sense, then."

"Isn't everything? My exhibition at the Kaiser Gallery in the Pearl District is solo. That means the gallery owner believes in my work—and believes I can draw in a crowd. The invitations have gone out for a private showing, a reception for the opening."

Cooper nodded, more curious than ever to see her work. "You have any photos on your cell?"

She gave a slight lift of her brow as if questioning his interest. Tugging out her cell phone, she opened up images of her paintings, then handed the phone over to Cooper. "I don't really like to do this. These photographs don't really..."

"Do them justice? I get that. But I want to see." He took her cell and stared at the images.

Unsure what to make of her paintings, he kept his face blank. He knew nothing of the art world, had never fully understood Jeremy's art, but what he saw—paintings of various animals such as an eagle, a polar bear, a peacock, each in their own paintings with weird distorted melding of landscapes in the background—dazed him at first. Overwhelmed him. Almost too creative for him to comprehend.

"They're beautiful." And he meant it. It just took him a few moments.

She laughed, but it sounded forced. "That's not what your expression said."

"They weren't what I expected. It took me a minute to figure things out. Give a guy a break."

Hadley snatched her cell away. He hoped he hadn't hurt her feelings. "I have some of the larger paintings in galleries," she said. "I have a following and—" she hung her head, and her next words were choked with tears "—and finally a national debut. I'm sure my father's connections had something to do with the national gallery, honestly."

Her father's connections...

Cooper cleared his throat. "I... I don't know much about the art world, but Hadley, those paintings are wonderful and sounds to me like you've done all the work on your own." The paintings *were* impressive. Hadley was amazing.

She dropped her head back to look at the sky, her eyes closed and her strawberry-blond hair cascading over her shoulders. He wanted to touch the curls. She was a beautiful creature of the forest, captivating him.

A tear streaked down her temple into her hair. Cooper pursed his lips, hating to see her cry, and yet grateful that she was letting him see just how vulnerable she was.

She turned her face to him, her smile both cynical and beautiful.

He climbed to his feet, held out his hand to her. "Come on, we need to get going."

He'd let them linger far too long, and the sun would set soon in the forests of the Siskiyou Mountains. Dusk would be darker in the woods as they made their way back to his vehicle. She took his hand and he helped her to her feet. She stood much too close, her eyes piercing his.

"It's my dream, you know—a national debut and this art show. There's a reception at the gallery. I'm expected to be there."

In that moment, Cooper wasn't sure he liked what he saw in her gaze. Determination wasn't always a good thing. "That was before you found out you have a contract out on your life. So I want to be clear that you shouldn't make plans to attend."

The light in her eyes, the hope he'd seen there, flickered then died.

And he felt the pain in his heart as if it had been his own. He'd overcome his own adversity to make his dreams come true. He understood what it would mean for her to miss this opportunity.

But he couldn't see a way to make it work for her to attend. His focus must remain on keeping her alive. Not making sure her dreams came true.

They climbed out of the waterfall hollow formed by the ridge and hiked back through the woods. Attuned to their surroundings, Cooper made sure they were alone and safe. Far away from her would-be assassins. He couldn't shake how deeply her disappointment had hurt him.

Though he wasn't close to knowing this woman well enough to fall for her, warning signals pounded through his thick skull. He could not let his heart get wrapped up in her. He had enough issues without getting caught up with a woman who preferred the finer things in life, especially considering her plans to hobnob in the highbrow art world. That was Hadley's world, and Cooper's world was here in the thick of the wilderness.

He had to keep his focus on helping her. And maybe his self-imposed mission had everything to do with saving someone when he was given the chance to make up for failing his brother. Failing his family. But even if he didn't have that dark past stalking him, he could never turn his back on this chance to right a wrong.

To see justice served.

And in saving Hadley, he had to do whatever it took to get her back to her world safe and sound, so that she could live there forever.

Far from him.

NINE

Cooper focused his tired eyes on the precarious one-lane mountain road—what he could see of it a few yards in front of him via his headlights.

Driving this dangerous road at night wasn't the wisest decision he'd ever made, but he sensed he needed to push through to get to the old cabin tonight. He had to put as much distance as possible between them and Hadley's assailant, getting them as deep into the wilderness as he could.

In a pinch, of course, he could build them a shelter. But he wanted to give Hadley a sense of security and stability, especially for these first few days of going off grid. Even though it was old and dilapidated, four solid walls and a roof would be more reassuring than any rudimentary shelter he could erect.

Normally, he would consider the measures he was taking to be overkill. But he'd fought two assassins sent to kill Hadley. Nothing he did to protect her would be in excess. So right now, they couldn't stop until they made the destination where he believed they would be safe.

Then he might be able to relax and make plans for their next step. Whatever that might be.

Next to him, Hadley remained tense, her wide eyes watching the road as if she could control his maneuvers by sheer will should he make a mistake and run them off the road and down a hundred-foot drop. Cooper got that—he felt the same way when he rode shotgun with anyone on roads like this.

The canopy of trees was thick around the road that hugged a rocky wall carved out of the mountain, leaving them in complete darkness except for the narrow beam of headlights. Hadley shivered.

Was she cold? He bumped up the heater. But he didn't think that was it.

She caught his glimpse her way and shot him a soft smile. "If it's all right with you, I'd really appreciate it if you would keep your eyes on the road."

He chuckled. "Yes, ma'am."

She shuddered again. "It's so eerie out here at night. I can't see a thing, except the tunnel your lights carve ahead of us."

"It's okay," he said. "I know my way around."

"Does anyone else ever drive this road?"

"A few people. But you're right. It's a mostly

untraveled back road through the wilderness and national forest. But the scenery is stunning. I hate that it's dark and you can't see it right now. But at some point you'll get the chance."

"I hope we don't meet someone coming from the other direction."

"Nah, that's not going to happen. People don't drive this road at night and rarely in the day."

"Unless they're in a mad rush to escape and hide from an assassin. I'm glad it's deserted…but it really doesn't seem to be well maintained. We already ran into a boulder but at least it hadn't blocked the whole road. But Cooper, what if that happens? Then what are we going to do? Go all the way back?"

"That's not going to happen to us." He shrugged. There was always the possibility, but he wasn't going to dwell on everything that might go wrong.

"Because you're the survival expert."

"I like to think I am." Even so, he had no control over fallen logs or boulders. The only thing he was ever in control of was his response to a situation.

"How much farther?"

"It's not that far, but it takes a long time to get there. I'm sorry it's so tedious. Why don't you get some rest? You can lean the seat back pretty far."

The curves in the road straightened out, letting Cooper see more than half a mile ahead.

He steered over an old rickety wooden truss bridge, also one lane, with a load-bearing limit of five tons. He hoped the bridge was stable, and he tensed as he drove onto it. He let the window down and instantly heard the roar of a much larger river. The Rogue carved out a rugged canyon within a complex terrain of ridges and cliffs. Though it was beautiful, he was almost glad they were driving over this bridge at night.

Hadley might be more terrified if she could really see where they were going.

His vehicle rocked over the uneven slats, and he could feel the tension rolling from Hadley. Her knuckles were likely white from gripping the handgrip. Finally, they had crossed the bridge, solid ground beneath the tires. He released a slow breath, hoping Hadley wouldn't notice.

Cooper didn't see the problem until she brought it up.

"Is that…are those car lights?"

Cooper shifted in his seat. "Sure are."

"They're coming toward us. Cooper, there isn't anywhere for us to go."

To Cooper's left was the razor-edged ridge and drop into the river. To his right, the Yukon was right up against the steep vertical ridge of carved-out rock of the mountain. The driver coming their way could pull over into a turnout, find a place where the road opened up no matter how narrow, but instead of pulling over, the vehicle's floodlights turned on, nearly blinding Cooper. The driver appeared to increase speed, the lights bouncing and shining in his eyes. And Cooper didn't like the speed at which the other vehicle was coming toward them.

He didn't like what he was about to do, but he had no choice. He stopped, shifted into Reverse, and started driving backward, with only the glow of his rear lights to guide him. The going was slower than he liked, but if he wasn't careful, he would back them right over the edge and into the river.

"This is crazy! What are you doing?"

"Focusing on driving."

"What's going on? Why does that driver keep coming?"

"Tell me, Hadley, is he getting closer?" Cooper couldn't afford to turn his head forward and look.

"Surely there are other measures in place for running into someone like this."

"There are. They're called turnouts. That driver probably had a place to stop and wait for us to pass, but he didn't stop. Now I have to back up."

"You could just stop and talk to him."

"I can, but I have a feeling his intentions aren't exactly friendly."

"A feeling? Coop, you don't think…"

"I don't know. Not taking any chances."

He certainly hadn't expected this.

The end of the bridge that spanned a portion of the Rogue River was just behind them. Beyond that, there was a turnout, if Cooper could just make it that far. But then what? If the driving of the person closing in on them was any indication, the turnout wouldn't save them.

"Cooper, he's getting closer." She'd started calling him by his full name again. That told him something.

He punched the accelerator and the vehicle rocked violently over the slats, jarring his teeth.

"Cooper!" Hadley screamed.

He turned to look forward just as the vehicle slammed into them. Airbags exploded. The other vehicle kept pushing, ramming them. He'd thought his Yukon was big, but the other driver's truck was built like a tank.

Next to him, Hadley gasped for breath. "What do we do?"

Cooper was glad to hear her voice, but had no idea how to reply to her question.

"I don't know!"

He had to stop this mad driver from killing them. Why was he always on the defensive? This had to stop. But Cooper couldn't regain control or steer, and his Yukon was pinned against the lame excuse for a guardrail.

Then the tail of his Yukon broke through, slipping off the bridge.

Floodlights shined into Hadley's face, blinding her, and spotlighting how vulnerable she was. Instinctively, she ducked. The airbags had now deflated and she shoved the material forward and off her legs as much as possible, then hunched lower in the seat.

They both needed to get out of here. But how? They were on a bridge. They couldn't run away. The floodlights left no place to hide.

Cooper's poor Yukon was half on, half off the bridge. No way would she sit here and wait.

"We have to get out of this before it goes over."

"I agree. I'm getting out first. I'll see if I can draw the driver's attention. Worst case, I'll shoot, and that will give you cover to get out."

"But my side is the one hanging. There's a narrow escape, but then nothing. What should I do?" She was scared, but didn't want Cooper to know if he hadn't already guessed.

"All right, then. Start climbing this way. But let me get out first. When I signal that it's safe, jump out and run to the backside of vehicle. Got it?"

"Got it."

Cooper opened his door and slid out. Instantly a round of bullets pelleted the door. The man wanted them to go over with the Yukon. Wanted to trap them inside, then push them over to their death.

Oh, God, no, please don't let this happen.

"Now, Hadley, go!" Cooper fired his weapon off as the vehicle continued to ram them.

The door tried to shut on her, pinning her in. Cooper shoved it open. "Go!"

She ducked, then slipped out and crept around to the back bumper. It shifted toward the edge of the bridge, but it was stuck, almost high-centered, and wouldn't budge. Hadley peered at the bridge where the wooden beams serving as guardrails had splintered and broken. Why hadn't they replaced this long ago with steel?

Hovering near the bumper, she risked a glance around the corner. "Cooper, come on!"

He fired off another round, then, leaving the door open to protect them, ran to Hadley. "I need to get the supplies out of the back. Can you cover me?"

"Why don't I grab the gear instead?"

"It's not stable enough. Not safe." He handed the weapon over.

Hadley wrapped her hand around the grip. She'd told him about her father taking her to the firing ranges, so Cooper knew she could handle the weapon. But this was very different from a firing range. She leaned forward, watching the other vehicle. The engine had stopped revving.

Did that mean the driver had gotten out? Was he making his way toward them now? Could he be circling Cooper's SUV, about to come up behind them?

"Cooper," she whispered. "You'd better hurry. Something has changed. I think he got out of the truck." He or she, but Hadley would bet on a he. This had to be an assassin sent to kill her. She could think of no other reason someone would attempt this.

"I'm here. Got the stuff." Cooper was right behind her with two large backpacks. "Not all of it, but this will have to do."

She handed the weapon back to him. "I'd like to have my own gun as well, if possible. I had planned to get one. Didn't get the chance."

"I packed more weapons, but we can dig them out later—we don't have time for that now."

He handed over her pack stashed with money. Thinking of lugging such a quantity of cash around with her left a sick feeling in her gut. Was it blood money? But she buried the thoughts for now when Cooper handed her another, bigger pack. "Put this one on. It holds survival stuff, unless you think your bag is more important."

"I can't leave my pack, I'm sorry."

Cooper frowned. He grabbed the extra pack and set it on the edge of the bridge.

"Where are we going?" she asked, keeping

her voice low. "We can't run across the bridge to safety—he'll see us and shoot us down.

The other vehicle started up again, the engine revved and rammed, jarring the Yukon enough to bump into Hadley. She fell forward and into Cooper who caught her.

"You okay?"

"Yeah, just startled me." Hadley sagged against him. Hating her momentary weakness. She'd have a bruise there for sure. "What are you thinking? What are we going to do? There isn't any escape."

"I think you're right. If we run the length of the bridge to the other side, he'll gun us down. He's pushing our only protection off the bridge now."

Cooper put some distance between him and the back of his vehicle. He glanced over the side. Besides the snapping and cracking of the wood on the bridge, and the revving and ramming of the other vehicle, Hadley could hear the river's roar as it rushed below them in its flow to the Pacific.

"I have an idea."

She didn't like the image his words conjured. "It had better not be what I think it is. I'm not jumping into the river."

"I'm not asking you to. We can climb beneath this old bridge and hang on to the trusses. Make our way across like that."

Hadley wasn't sure she could swallow past the knot in her throat. "I don't know if I can do that."

"I've seen you fight. You've got good, strong arms. You're small. You can hold your body weight and then some. It's our only choice."

Cooper climbed over the side and looked at her. "But you have to hurry before he sees us."

This is insane!

The Yukon rocked. Wood splintered and metal crunched as more of the vehicle inched over the edge of the bridge.

"Hadley, we've got to go now. Now!" Then Cooper disappeared into the darkness and the shadows of the bridge.

Hadley wanted to close her eyes, to squeeze them shut like she might on a roller coaster until the scary part was over. But that wouldn't do here. Even though it was dark, she needed her eyes open. She lifted her leg and climbed over the railing, her hands gripping despite the sliver that slid under her skin.

Her feet still on the bridge, she wasn't sure what to do next.

"Hadley." Cooper tugged her pant leg. "Down here. Just slide down and catch the edge of the beam. Get a good grip. We're going to crawl on these."

"I can't see a thing, the floodlights are still too bright, and the shadows are too dark."

"Don't worry. I've got you. This is like the monkey bars or a jungle gym in school."

"Yeah, well, I never played on those."

"That's too bad."

Was he trying to force levity into this? Because it was not working. Hadley's feet were on the bottom of the wooden beam now and she stretched down and felt for a handhold.

Cooper reached up and grabbed the extra pack she carried—the one he'd prepped for her, since she was still carrying the one from her father—and let it drop.

"What…what are you doing?"

Seconds later, they heard what could have been the bag's splash as the roar of the river consumed it, but it was hard to discern. Maybe she'd imagined the splash.

"I'll try to recover it downstream. But I can't carry it and you, too."

"Me? You're not carrying me, I've got this."

"Good. Now, grab a hold—a good strong grip and let yourself hang. Use your legs where the beams let you. We have to cover the distance beneath the bridge. Stay focused and on task."

She'd spoken too soon. *I don't know if I can do this.*

Cooper must have sensed her hesitation. "Just focus on putting one arm in front of the other and let's get across. I've seen you in action, Hadley. I know you can do this."

And then what? Arm over arm she'd make

her way across and cover the distance, knowing a river raged beneath her? These had to be the worst options. But none of that mattered. He was right. She needed to focus on one thing—getting to safety.

Hadley did her best not to think about the fact she was hanging over white water rapids. She tried not to think about how far she'd fall if she dropped. It was all she could do to focus on taking slow, even breaths.

With each reach, each grip of the beam, her muscles strained and screamed. Despite the drop in temperature, sweat poured from her body. She had too far to go and she was overtaxing her strength already.

The Yukon crunched and protested and finally, slipped from the edge, pulling a chunk of the railing and edge of the truss with it. Hadley squeezed her eyes shut, hunkered behind a beam and held on tight, while trying to stifle a scream. This time, they heard the definitive splash and clank of metal twisting against granite boulders as the vehicle fought with the ravenous river.

"Hadley, you okay?" Cooper's voice broke through the cacophony.

A few seconds passed and the sound subsided to the normal roar.

"Let's go," Cooper said.

He inched on, but she could tell he was holding back, moving slowly so he wouldn't leave her behind. Hadley moved beneath the bridge at a crawl but here, where the beams crisscrossed, she could use her legs, too. Still, her fingers ached and palms burned with the effort. The wooden girders were nothing like the smooth metal of the monkey bars she had never played on.

Above them, the driver shut off his engine, but the floodlights still shined on the bridge. Cooper stopped moving and Hadley followed his lead.

Other than the river rushing below them, the night had turned eerily quiet.

Clunk, clunk, clunk.

Their pursuer clomped along the bridge searching for them. Did he think they'd gone over with the SUV? Hadley held her breath. Didn't move. But she couldn't keep hanging here forever. They needed to traverse the underpinnings of the bridge to the other side, but moving might give them away. Between the wooden slats of the bridge, she could just make out their attacker's form.

He moved to where the SUV had plummeted and looked out into the darkness. Hadley swallowed and could swear the sound had caught his attention. He twisted from the edge of the bridge and got on his knees to peer through the smallest of spaces between the slats and looked right at Hadley.

TEN

Don't you scream! Don't blink. Don't breathe. Don't...move.

Hadley reacted like she could hear Cooper's thoughts, except for one thing—her breaths came louder and faster.

A millisecond later she grunted and scrambled along the girder, closer to Cooper.

Their pursuer had discovered them. Gunfire pelted the bridge, but couldn't penetrate. Now they were on the race of their lives. The man climbed over the side of the bridge just as Cooper and Hadley had done. Cooper saw his silhouette as he hung down, aiming to fire.

Cooper repositioned himself, grabbed his own weapon and returned fire.

The man released a string of curses and hid behind a beam.

"Hadley," Cooper hissed. "Are you hit?"

"No."

"Keep going. I'll cover you."

"I don't know if I can make it, I'm sorry. My hands need a rest."

There was no chance for that now.

So their attacker wouldn't get any ideas about moving closer, Cooper fired off more rounds, but he was about to run out of ammo. He wasn't exactly in the right position to get to the extra ammo he'd packed. If his goal was to keep Hadley alive and get her to safety, he was failing miserably.

Acid burned in his gut. Moisture slicked over his body and his palms. "Okay, Plan B."

"You mean there was another option?"

"Not really. I wouldn't consider Plan B an option. It's a matter of no options."

"You're the survival guy. I'm putting my trust in you."

A bullet whizzed by his ear, slammed into the girder.

Out of time. "Listen to me. We can't make it this way. We have to drop."

A series of shuddering gasps reached his ears. Was she hyperventilating?

"You mean…into the river?"

"Yes."

"What about the rocks? What about the rapids and drowning?"

Gunfire resounded and a trail of bullets slammed into the beam near Hadley's head. She screamed.

Cooper fired his own weapon, sending the jerk back under cover.

"Right now I'd rather take my chances with the river than stick around here. We've moved closer to the center of the bridge now and where the river's deeper. Fewer rocks. Our chances are better."

"So I can choose between the bullets or the river? Those aren't choices, Cooper. You have to do something. Crawl over there and shoot him or something."

"I'm nearly out of rounds," he whispered. "I've got more in my bag, but I can't get to them like this. Dropping into the river is our only choice."

"But it's dark. I can't see anything. I couldn't even dodge the rocks if I wanted to."

"Float on your back, feet first, and go with it. I'll drop first, then you. That will give me a better chance of helping you."

More gasping.

"Hadley?"

"Yes?"

"Are we good?"

"No. We're not good."

"Hang on, I'm coming over to you."

The man after them was repositioning himself. Coming at them from another angle. Cooper figured he had seconds, not minutes, to get to her. The river could save them or kill them, but they were not going to make it out of this alive without jumping.

When he crawled next to Hadley, he heard her trying to hide her whimpers. "I don't think I can hold on any longer, anyway," she admitted.

He took off his pack and let it drop. It was too heavy and would hold him down in the river. Worst case, he could survive without it—after all, he staked his business on it. Now he was staking his life on it.

And then he realized it—wasn't this what he had prepared for all these years? In that same way he knew when danger was imminent, that sixth sense that raised the hair on his arms and neck, deep down he'd known a day would come when he would need to put his survival skills to use in the real world.

Then he started removing Hadley's pack. "What… What are you doing?"

"Coming to help you. The pack will drag you down in the river."

"But…the things my father packed for me will get ruined." She hadn't exactly told Cooper what was in the pack that was so important. He had his theories.

"It's a dry pack. Your father thought of that much at least. Now, let go of it."

She let him slip it from her shoulders and then he dropped it.

"We're jumping together. Take my hand." Cooper fought not to think of it as a suicide jump. This couldn't end like that. He wouldn't let it.

Once Hadley gripped him, he said, "On the count of three let go, and wrap your arms around me. Try not to scream. I don't want him realizing we've jumped and firing into the river. Got it?"

"Got it."

"One… Two… Three." She released the girder and grabbed him just as he let go of the bridge and held tight to Hadley. Held on for dear life.

Despite his warning, they both cried out into the night. Dropping into the darkness terrified Cooper more than he wanted to admit. Somewhere behind them he heard gunfire echoing through the ravine.

He squeezed Hadley to him.

"It's okay. It's okay. It's okay." He spoke into her ear, the words for him as much as for her.

Cooper sent up a silent prayer. *God, be with us!*

"No matter what happens, try to hang on to me." Cooper braced himself for what would come next. "Take a breath!"

Icy cold, rushing water engulfed them, dragging them under.

The black, freezing water rushed over and around her, and tried to pull her away from Cooper. Holding her breath, clinging to him with all her strength, she squeezed her eyes shut, praying with everything inside her. Hoping that God would listen to her silent screams.

The river had a plan of its own, and the force of rushing water proved too much for Hadley, whose arms were torn away from Cooper. She grappled, water swooshing her body around like a rag doll, flailing, reaching for Cooper. He kept a grip on her at first, but suddenly water rushed between them and ripped him away.

No, Cooper! No!

The force swirled around her and dragged her under. Boulders slid past her body, raking over her back, bumping her head and her thrashing limbs.

Oh, God, oh, God, oh, God...

I don't want to die!

Craving air, her lungs burned. She flailed as her body was twirled and thrown about. If she didn't reach the surface soon, Hadley knew she would drown.

What had Cooper said?

Stay on her back? Legs first? Don't fight the river. Fat chance.

Hadley wasn't even sure which direction was up. Disoriented, she found her sense of bearing was distorted, but she thrust with her legs and her arms, hoping—praying—for the surface. Finally, the water's surface broke away from her face and air met her skin. Before she was dragged under again, Hadley pulled in a breath. She tried to lie on her back and stop fighting. Moonlight bathed the landscape in eerie silver and brought the canyon and river alive. Now she could see the boulders and the riverbank.

Except, there was no bank. Nothing but rock walls on all sides.

"Cooper! Cooper, where are you?" He'd thought if they jumped together and held tight, they would be able to stick together. Instead, they'd been pulled apart by a force beyond their control.

It reminded her of her father and all that had happened. The Rogue River rushed forward at a dizzying speed. Her arms and legs grew numb until she couldn't control them. Keeping her head above water became her only thought.

Seconds turned to minutes until finally, Hadley felt the current slowing. She tried to direct herself closer to the bank, now that she saw one, but her arms would not cooperate. There wasn't enough strength in them to battle the river.

The simple act of staying afloat became too ·difficult to manage, and she slipped under the water. Desperate, she urged her head above the water again.

Just a little longer. Stay alive, just a little longer.

"Hadley!"

Cooper's voice rang out. She spewed water and gasped. "Cooper, where are you? Cooper!"

"Hadley, keep calling out. I'll find you."

She called his name. Cried out for him. But she heard nothing more. "God, help us get out of this river."

She dipped under and couldn't seem to push her face up this time. She was lost forever. Would run out of air soon.

Would facing the assassin's bullets have been a better way to die?

Strong arms swooped around her, tugged her up until she could drag in a breath. "I've got you."

Cooper pulled her close and tugged her along with him. How? How could he still have strength in his arms? In his legs, his extremities, to swim them toward the riverbank? How was it that the icy cold hadn't disabled him as it had her? She felt weak. Helpless. And so very grateful for Cooper that she nearly broke down in tears. She hadn't been strong enough to save herself. But it didn't matter. Because Cooper, with God's help, had saved her yet again. She let him pull her along, relishing in the fact they had survived the river. When her legs felt the bottom, Cooper assisted her to her feet. Gulping in air, they clung to each other like they'd wanted to in the river, and plodded forward in the shallow water that beat softly against the bank of a small cove between the rocks.

Hadley fell to her knees and Cooper joined her. He rolled to his back and sucked in the cool night air. Hadley pressed her head forward into the pebbles and wet sand.

Behind her lids, tears flooded her eyes.

"Thank You, God," she whispered. Finally, Hadley rolled onto her back and stared at the stars. The only sound audible was the river rushing by in a mad frenzy a mere feet away from them. "And…thank you, Cooper."

Shivering, she scraped her wet hair from her face. She'd lost her cap to the river.

He sat up and stared at her.

"Are we still in danger?" She wasn't sure she wanted to know the answer.

"More so from the cold than from our attacker at the moment. He knows to look for us downstream, but looking for us at night would be too hazardous even with night-vision goggles. Not like he can climb down into the canyon at night. And even if he did, he wouldn't know exactly where to look." Cooper turned his gaze to the river, the canyon and then the night sky. "We have a head start on him, and we don't want to lose that."

"How did he do that, Cooper? How did he find us and come from the other direction?"

"There's a tracking device somewhere. Simple enough to see where we're headed and come at us from the opposite direction. Easier than trying to catch us. I'm thinking he might have had some help, too, finding the right roads. Some of the ones we took aren't on the maps or GPS."

"Oh, no. I hope that doesn't mean he's hurt someone else to get to me."

Cooper shrugged, but said nothing. Hadley envisioned the assassin forcing someone who knew the region well to map out a path and killing them. She hated the image accosting her mind, her heart. Hoped it wasn't true.

Hadley shook her head. She'd never been good at word problems. "Even so...how?"

"He made better time taking the freeway around the wilderness region, planning to cut us off on the other side. So he found a mountain road and came at us from the opposite direction. He knew he had a better chance of catching us that way."

"Why didn't we take the highway, too, if it was faster?"

"We were trying to get lost and avoid being seen, remember? Going back to civilization would have meant exposing ourselves. What we need to figure out now is where is the tracking device? Because there is absolutely no other way he could have found us here. You don't happen to still have your cell, do you?"

She dragged one out of her pocket, sopping wet. "It's no use to us now."

"I wasn't thinking of calling anyone. A hacker

can track you through your phone, though it wouldn't be easy out here where there are no towers." Cooper took the phone and pulled it apart and crushed the pieces.

At Hadley's surprised look, he said, "Just in case." Then he stood and offered his hand.

Hadley pressed hers in his palm and let him pull her to her feet. She desperately wanted to lean into him, needing to soak up the warmth she knew would be emanating from his body despite his wet, cold clothes.

"Coop," she whispered and finally gave in to her need. She stepped closer until her body was next to him. "This is... I just need to get warm."

He wrapped his arms around her and tugged her nice and close. It felt like much more than two people simply getting warm. The heat made her realize just how cold she was. If only they had their packs—surely he'd brought blankets. A tent. Some sort of shelter. A sizzling fire would be nice right about now.

"How do we ever escape this?"

"We're heading deeper into a designated wilderness area. That plan hasn't changed."

"Then we'll wait him out?"

"I'm not sure yet."

"At least you're being honest with me, admitting that you don't really have a plan."

He stiffened. "I *do* have a plan, Hadley. Sometimes things change and you have to change with them. You have to be flexible."

Not wanting to argue, she simply snuggled closer and he shifted, running his hand over her head, weaving his fingers between strands of her wet hair. Exhaustion had destroyed her defenses. It was the only explanation for how much she liked the feel of his arms around her. The only reason she didn't have the strength to step away from him. She reminded herself the only man in her life before Cooper had been her father and look at the secret he'd kept from her. She believed that Cooper was being honest with her—but that didn't mean she was ready to trust him or anyone else with her heart. It was difficult enough trusting him with her life.

Cooper eased her head back.

His face inches from hers, moonlight illuminated his strong features. "Are you okay?"

"If you're asking if I'm warm enough, I don't know if I'll ever be truly warm again."

"Hadley," he whispered.

She could barely make out his gaze, but something stirred behind his eyes and ricocheted inside. No. Nothing was happening between them. Nothing *could* happen. She was in his arms now to bring her body heat up and *that* was the only reason.

"I'm good, Coop." She tried to step free, but her body betrayed her with a shiver.

In response, Cooper pulled her close again, and she didn't resist. She couldn't.

"What about your packs, Coop? What about mine? How are we going to find them?"

"I'm hoping at least one of them washed to the bank the same as we did. I thought… I thought I'd lost you back there, Hadley." The depth of emotion in his voice surprised her. "I'm sorry about this turn of events. Do you still trust me?"

She would trust him with helping her through this, but that was where her trust stopped. "None of this was your fault. You've kept me alive this far and it isn't even your fight. Yes, I still trust you."

"Good, because there's no turning back now."

ELEVEN

"There."

Cooper lugged the dripping pack—Hadley's pack, from her father—out of the rocky outcropping, which captured it from the river and held it in place.

So far, it was the only one of their bags he could find. She appeared anxious to get her hands on it so Cooper tossed it at her feet.

Relief swept across her features when she peered inside.

"I don't suppose that has anything we can actually use in it."

She glanced up at him. "No, sorry. What about the other bags? Are you going to search for them?"

"I already have. They must be farther downriver, but we can't afford to waste time looking."

"But…do we need them to survive?"

His boot soggy, he stepped on a large flat boulder and considered her question. "No. I brought supplies to make it easier, but we can manage without them." He sure wished they had them, though. Not just the food or the camping supplies, but his waterproof cell phone, too. What good did it do to have one, if you were going to lose it in the dunk?

"Not that I'm opposed to roughing it or anything, but please tell me we can get more supplies." Her voice hitched.

Wanting to reassure her, Cooper grabbed her hand and led her forward. They could talk as they hiked and movement would warm them up. "Of course we can if we're careful about it. But everything depends on how long we're going to stay. How long your life will remain in danger."

Their attackers were relentless. Cooper thought they could hide out in the wilderness, but doubt gnawed at him now. Still, it was their only choice if they wanted a chance to catch their breath and think everything through before they made any fatal mistakes.

He hated to admit that he'd already made several mistakes, and they had almost been fatal. He hadn't expected the assassin to show up so quickly at his shop, and not at all on the bridge, and he hadn't expected they would have to jump for their lives into a hazardous river. It had become obvious with each attempt on Hadley's life their margin of error was narrow. Cooper might have underestimated both men that had come for her so far.

Or…had the tally gone up to three?

"Hadley, did you get a look at him?"

"The guy on the bridge? Yes, when he looked at me through the slats. Why?"

"So was he the same guy in the shop?"

She nodded. "I don't think I'll ever forget those eyes."

Cooper let that news settle in. It didn't matter either way. Regardless of how many killers were out there, his plans would remain the same for now.

At least the moon gave them light, casting peculiar, dappled shadows through the dark forest as Cooper kept up his pace. Though he had great night vision, he still concentrated on their path and listened to the night sounds with a keen ear.

"How much farther?" Hadley asked. "Where exactly are we going? I thought you could survive anywhere. Why don't we make a camp here?"

Her voice resounded through the forest and silence rippled in response.

Quiet. Cooper paused and turned so she could see his profile. He held a finger to his lips. Hadley brushed up against him, whether out of fear or in need of warmth, he wasn't sure. He wrapped his arm around her. He could tell she wanted to speak, but he remained unmoving, listening.

Finally the night sounds—frogs croaking before the temperature dropped too low, a coyote or two, raccoons and other insects, and even an owl—came back to life. Hadley sagged against him.

She leaned in close. "You never answered my questions."

"Trying to put some distance between us. We have more to worry about than black bears and rattlesnakes in these woods." There was the constant threat of an assassin finding them.

"Wait. Bears and snakes?"

"Did you think you could hike a wilderness region without dangerous animals?"

"I guess I hadn't really thought about it."

"Don't worry, Hadley. I teach wilderness survival, remember? I have a place in mind where we can get out of the elements, away from the animals, and rest. You're going to be fine."

"So why don't you give me some wilderness survival tips? That will get my mind off how tired I am. Maybe off the attempts on my life."

Good idea. "My training uses a combination of skills I learned in the military, modern survival skills and also Native American skills. The more you know and the stronger you are, the better your chances to not only survive, but to potentially live well, or thrive."

"Live well out here? I'm listening."

"First, you have three survival priorities. Can you guess what they are?"

"Food, water and shelter."

"Yes. You can survive for three hours without the required core body temperature. Too hot or too cold for too long, and you'll die. Three days is the longest you can go without water. And three weeks without food, give or take. People who die in the wilderness usually die because they were too cold or too hot. Dehydration is the second most common cause of death."

"So you're saying find shelter first, then water? I always thought water was the priority."

"Finding shelter near water is good, but shelter is your top priority. Now, if you find yourself without your gear like us, it's easy to make a shelter with leaves and sticks. You've probably seen enough movies to know sticks can be rubbed together creating enough friction to make a fire. But, and you in particular will find this funny, Native American wisdom is to make art with your tools, too."

"Huh? Oh…okay."

"You've seen ornate Native American survival tools somewhere, I'll wager. The thinking is that if you put a lot of time and effort in to the details of even building a fire, you'll have a better, longer-lasting fire. Put thought into building a shelter, then it will keep you warmer. Make sense?"

"Totally, Cooper. So I guess maybe you and I have something in common?"

"Yeah? What's that?"

"You're an artist, too, so to speak, only your medium is different."

He smiled at that but then let his smile drop. He hoped she wasn't making a list of things they had in common.

What was worse, the thought made his heart jump. "I guess you're right."

A branch cracked, echoing through the woods. Cooper paused and held Hadley close. When he heard no other sounds he urged her forward, but put a finger to his lips. They should keep quiet for now as they kept hiking toward their destination. Making noise would chase away the bears and other dangerous animals, but he was more worried about the assassin.

They hiked for what seemed like days, though it was only a couple of hours. Cooper and Hadley almost sagged against each other as they continued marching forward until finally, through the trees, he spotted the place where he should find shelter—only because he knew to look for it. He pulled her forward, new energy in his steps. When he made the bottom of the cliff and looked up into the shadows, relief rushed through him. They had made it to the berm cabin built into the side of a cliff. He stared at the shadows, aware that Hadley was watching him. She didn't see what he saw in the dark. Most people wouldn't, which was the advantage he was counting on. The only disadvantage was they could get trapped inside with no escape.

"Come on, let's go."

He hiked toward the ridge, careful where he stepped. This would have been so much better with his supplies, but at least they were here now.

"What are we doing? Where are we going?"

"Don't you see it?"

Shaking her head, she squinted her eyes.

Cooper pulled her into the shadows and pressed her hand against the door. "What about now?"

"It's a cabin. But…"

"It's partly built into this cliffside. There's a cave at the back."

"Here? We're going to stay here?"

"You were expecting something different?"

"I don't know."

"I hope you have a flashlight in your bag."

"Me? Why would you think that?"

"Matches?"

"My bag doesn't have that kind of stuff."

"You carry it around like your life depends on it so I thought maybe it had survival supplies." Though she'd already told him that it didn't, he'd held on to hope for at least something useful.

She didn't respond.

Fine. Cooper would ask her about it later. He eased open the door. Moonlight streamed through a portion of the front room, but it would fall behind the opposing cliff face and they would be in the dark for most of the rest of the night. "At least we'll be warmer in here than outside. This cabin uses the cliff as three sides of the walls and will keep out the cold pretty effectively."

"It's kind of like a hobbit house."

He chuckled. "I guess you could say that."

"Sounds like you've been here often."

"Not often, no. Gray discovered it. It's on Bureau of Land Management—BLM—property, and is abandoned so it's a good place to take shelter from the elements in an emergency."

"Like now."

"Yes. I could have built a shelter for us, sure, but why would I when I knew this was here, and you'd feel more comfortable. Plus, we needed to get as far from our entry point out of the river as possible."

"Do you think he'll find us here?"

"I doubt it. But if he does, we're in trouble. We can only escape from the front."

Hadley found the small table against the wall and set her pack there. She slid into an old wobbly chair and immediately jumped up, gasping. "What's that?"

Cooper focused on the small creature racing

to the shadows. "A black widow spider. Beautiful creatures, but they can be deadly."

He hated to kill it but they couldn't risk running into it again. He quickly smashed it. Chances were good there were more inside, but without light he couldn't search the place for more spiders or other little troublemakers. Since they were only in autumn now, the rattlesnakes would still be outside but on cold days like today, they'd gather in the rocky places, caves, ridges and crevices. Not a comforting thought just now considering the berm cabin's location.

As for black bears, wouldn't it be something if a bear had taken up residence in the back cavern part? But he kept that thought to himself. He kept it all to himself. They didn't need even one more thing to go wrong.

Hadley shuddered and lifted her shoulders, glancing around the room. "Are you sure it's better to stay in here instead of outside?"

"What do you think?"

"I guess you're right. There could be bears and even more spiders out there."

Cooper was glad he kept his earlier thoughts to himself. He'd search the back of the cabin on his own on the small chance he'd disturb a bear or a congregation of rattlesnakes.

"So, we're good, then. You okay to sleep here tonight?"

"Yes. I guess."

Beggars can't be choosers. He held his tongue. It wasn't like she acted like she wanted a four-star hotel, and he was the one who'd dragged her out here to begin with. All his plans had been dashed on that bridge. The doubt that had plagued him since his brother's death chipped away at him now. But falling prey to his insecurities over the past wouldn't help keep Hadley alive. It no longer mattered if he were up to the task. They were here. He was it.

Aware she stared at him, he shook off his distracting thoughts and focused on getting them settled for the night.

"It's not stocked with food, sorry, but there should be some blankets. There's an old cot in the next room. I'll drag it out here where at least you have the moonlight for a while."

He made his way into the space off the main room and barely spotted the cot in the darkness. Lifting it, he shook it and scraped his hands over and around the bottom to knock off any spiders, then brought it out for Hadley.

Cooper situated the cot against the wall, then found the blankets and shook them out. "Get some rest."

"What about you?"

"I'll be fine."

"We can take turns watching."

He grinned. "I like your spunk, Hadley. You've

got spirit. Most people would be whining and complaining in this situation, but not you."

"Just because I'm not vocal about wishing we could stay someplace nicer doesn't mean I'm not feeling it on the inside."

Though he couldn't see her face, he could hear the smile in her words. Something warm tugged his own insides. He needed to pull back. "You hungry?"

"I could eat, but we lost our food."

"Unless you have food in your pack, yes, we did. But there are plenty of edible plants. And I could hunt. I still have my knife." And his semi-automatic but without any rounds. He'd need to pull it apart, clean it and let it dry before using it anyway. Funny he'd lost his cell and not his gun. "But on second thought, hunting would take longer plus I don't want to start a fire to cook and give our hiding place away."

She left the chair and tried out the cot. Wrapped the blanket around her and released a sigh. At least she was warm; now to get her fed. Frustration raked over him. She still wasn't giving up what was so important in her pack. How could Cooper have been such an idiot? Was there something in the pack that the assassin wanted? No, that couldn't be right—if the assassin had wanted the pack, he'd have demanded they turn it over.

Instead, it seemed he simply wanted to kill her. It was business. Kill and get paid.

"What is it?" She sat up straight.

"Nothing. I'll be back in a few minutes."

He made some noise, threw some rocks deeper, as he searched the back of the cabin where the rock walls of the cave served as part of the cabin enclosure, hoping he wouldn't stumble on anything in the dark, but he disturbed no bears or snakes. Then he left Hadley inside, easing out the door, alert to every sound and shadowy movement. Gripping his knife, he stayed in the shadows himself. Before he settled in for the night, he needed to make sure they had not been followed. Once he was certain, he'd gather a few edible plants—roots, weeds, mushrooms and wild fruit—whatever he could find. This wasn't the optimal situation. Building a fire would be much better—they'd be able to see inside the cabin and cook their dinner and dry out their clothes and stay warm. Plus, the fire would scare off animals. But that wasn't an option, when they were trying to avoid being spotted.

He crept around the area surrounding the cliff and cabin, continuing to watch and listen. Wishing he could curl up in a warm blanket by a fire instead.

He'd thought he could whisk her away and

they would be safe in the wilderness, but the man had found them near the bridge at a place he never should have followed—given the infinite possibilities of places Cooper could have taken them. Though her phone had been destroyed, if the device had even been the reason they had been found, Cooper didn't want to take any more chances. He needed to make sure the tracking device wasn't in her bag. That meant checking her for it whether she liked it or not.

Whether a tracking device was giving them away now or not, the assassin would continue to search for them. He knew they were in the wilderness region. But the question remained—would the assassin continue to search for them at night? In Special Forces, as a Green Beret, Cooper had participated in his share of unconventional warfare operations, including manhunts and it made no difference whether it was night or day.

The thought of it had him on edge.

The gray of dawn broke through Hadley's lids. She shifted uncomfortably, then realized she wasn't in her own soft bed. Scraping the hair from her face, she pushed up on her elbows, then the cot and rough blanket registered in her thoughts. Squinting her bleary eyes, she glanced around the room and sucked in a breath.

The events of yesterday crashed through her mind. *Oh, my... I thought it was just an awful dream.*

But wait. Had she slept all night? She was supposed to relieve Cooper. Where was he?

Hadley sat up and put her socked feet on the dusty floor. She started to call out his name but caught herself as images of fighting the man sent to kill her nearly choked her fully awake. Cooper had told her last night to keep quiet so she wouldn't give away their position. That could still be the case this morning, especially if the assassin had been searching all night.

Noiselessly, she put her boots on, wrapped the blanket around her shoulders, then moved around the small but ample berm structure looking for Cooper. He wasn't here. Had he gone in search of breakfast?

Her stomach rumbled, and she could use water to wet her dry, parched mouth. He'd given her some strange, end-of-the-season berries last night and some earthy-tasting mushrooms. She hadn't wanted to eat them, but he assured her he knew what he was doing and the mushrooms were edible. But all she could think about this morning was water. She knew little about survival but even before his brief lesson the previous night, she knew that much—water was necessary for life. She could go for weeks without eating, but not without water.

After a glimpse out the small window, Hadley confirmed Cooper wasn't close. Now was the perfect time to check the pack. Make sure the money hadn't gotten wet or ruined along with her passport. She'd noticed the way Cooper continued to eye the bag. It was obvious that he wanted to know what was in it, but she was afraid of his reaction to the money. Hadley dug inside and found her fake passport safe and dry as were the bills. She'd yet to actually count the money but knew by looking it was a significant amount. Then she spotted a small envelope.

How…how could she have missed that before?

She'd give herself a break. She'd been running for her life and hadn't exactly gone over everything with a fine-tooth comb. She slipped the envelope out, hoping Cooper wouldn't return too soon, though she hoped he wouldn't be gone too long, either, and would return bearing something edible, along with water.

She opened the envelope and read the elegant scrawl belonging to her CIA father. Anger and resentment surged followed by unshed tears. She hated the turmoil she felt over him. She *loved* him.

Hadley,
By now, the worst-case scenario is alive and

well in your life. I never wanted you to know about my work with the CIA because I want you to have every opportunity to make your own life. But if I've given this to you, then it's time now for a new life. Take the cash and passport. Use them to disappear and get somewhere safe before whoever has taken me out finds and kills you. And then when you are safe and no one has followed you, I want you to contact Ronny Pager who will help you leave the country. Trust no one else. With Ronny's help you can start over with your dream under your new name.

Never give up your dream. Make me proud of you, with all your accomplishments.

I love you, Hadley. I know it might not seem that way now, but you're strong. I know you will survive.

A phone number was scrawled at the bottom of the page—presumably the number for this Ronny Pager. Hadley couldn't focus on that, though, not when the rest of the letter was still running through her mind.

When Hadley pressed the envelope against her heart her skin felt seared. *My dream? Was he crazy? How can I live my dream when someone is trying to kill me? How can I create when all I see in my head is my father dying in that chair?*

Hadley stuffed everything back into the pack and plopped in the chair, wishing she was someone else living somewhere else. The irony. Her father had given her the chance to do just that. What would Cooper think of the letter? Would he help her contact this person? Her father had initially told her to trust no one, but perhaps he'd meant in her escape from Portland until she could contact this Ronny Pager.

She huffed a laugh.

Was that even his real name—Ronny Pager?

All she knew was that she couldn't hide out in the wilderness for the rest of her life. She couldn't live with this hanging over her head. She needed someone to help her find answers—that was the only way to end this mess.

Footfalls clomped near the door. Hadley stiffened. Instinctively looked for a weapon even though she hoped and believed it was Cooper.

He stepped through the door and set his bounty on the table. "Wild pears and muscadine grapes. They're kind of sweet for my taste but I'm just glad to have found them. It's near the end of the season." He plucked one of the big dark and plump grapes and popped it into his mouth. "You need to eat up."

"Exotic. I was expecting some unidentifiable

tubers and tree bark. This has me absolutely giddy!" She laughed, hoping he knew she was teasing. "Thanks, Coop. Really, I appreciate this."

"Eat quickly. We have to leave."

"I thought we were staying here. This place isn't as safe as you thought?"

"I know about the money, Hadley."

She gasped. "You looked inside my bag?"

"Yes. This is life or death. I had to know."

"You could have asked."

"And what would you have said?"

He was right and she knew it. Righteous indignation faded and she slumped a little. "I'm sorry I didn't tell you. I was afraid of what you would think. What you would say. That you wouldn't believe me about all this, thinking I stole the money. It was part of my father's provision."

"You were afraid that I would take the money myself, weren't you?" Anger flickered in his eyes and then it was gone. "No, never mind. It doesn't matter. I also found this." He up a small black square between his fingers, then placed it on the table.

"What is it?"

"What do you think?"

"Is that how he found us?"

"Yes. Some sort of long-range tracking device, I think."

"Is it working now?"

"He's probably using an app on his cell to track us down."

"Why don't you throw it in the river or destroy it?" Without waiting for his answer, Hadley grabbed her pack and strapped it on. "You're right, we need to leave and now. How…how and when did he do this?"

"My guess is that when he shot your father, he had access then to put the tracker in the backpack."

"That makes sense." She grabbed the small device and dropped it to the floor to crush it.

Cooper stopped her. Bent down and picked it up. He dropped it back in the pack. "I've been thinking."

"I'm not sure that's a good idea."

"We need to use this to our advantage. You don't want to spend the rest of your life running and hiding, do you?"

"Of course not." She already had plans to change that, but had no guarantees that she could even trust her father's contact or that he would help her.

"Then let's draw the assassin to us. This time, we'll be ready. Be proactive and take the offensive."

"Are you crazy? You've already battled him twice now. You had your chance. We crush this thing and we could lose him forever."

"Do you really believe that, Hadley? What about your dream? Don't you want your dream back?"

Her father's words jumped from the letter and took a bite out of her. *Never give up your dreams*.

"Of course, but it seems…impossible."

"Maybe together we can make it possible. Will you trust me?"

She shrugged, but again thought of the letter her father had left in the pack, and the Mr. Pager that he mentioned. "What's your plan?"

"I need time to think it through. To strategize." Cooper's voice had an odd strain to it, then he glanced out the door, looking anxious to leave.

"I think we've had all the time we're going to get, Cooper."

"If we can catch him maybe we can somehow force the information out of him," Cooper said. "Find out who is behind the contract on your life."

"And just how do you plan to *catch* him? Are you going to build a snare with your knife?"

Cold spilled from his eyes.

"Okay, I'm sorry. That was uncalled for. So say you catch him. What are you going to do then? Torture him to get your answers? Then we're no better than he is."

"Of course I wouldn't do that. But once we find out who hired him we can follow that lead and end this for good. So what do you think?"

"I think you're crazy," she admitted. "But maybe just crazy enough to be on to something."

"Until we figure this out, we have to keep moving and stay ahead of him. Unless he took a dunk in the river, too, it would have taken him hours to get to our starting point on the bank, so we have a bit of a lead. But now we need to get going."

Hadley glanced around the cozy cabin. In the light of morning, she could see potential, and now that she thought about it, hated to leave.

"Are we staying in the wilderness?"

"That remains to be seen. I just know we can't linger in one place too long." Cooper strode through the door.

And Hadley, of course, would follow. She pulled on the backpack, her thoughts returning again to the letter inside. She felt guilty for not sharing it with Cooper. He was risking his life for her. She needed to tell him about the letter, but a tingle crawled over her. A sense of foreboding. She'd wait until he got her to safety. Some place where she could walk out on her own, if needed.

A strange, whistling sound filled the air.

Cooper yanked her away from the berm and shoved her into the woods, covering her with his own body, just as the concussive force of an explosion rocked through her, shoving them hard against the ground.

TWELVE

A rocket launcher?

Rocks and debris tumbled. Cooper's ears rang. He covered Hadley, careful not to hurt her, until he was sure everything had settled. But he couldn't wait until the dust had cleared. They had to get out of here.

Had the assassin seen their escape?

"Hadley, are you okay?" In reply, words formed on her lips, but he couldn't hear them.

She tried to push up so he let her, then grabbed her hand.

"Run!" He wasn't sure if Hadley heard him, but she ran with him, understanding his actions.

He led her deeper into thick woods, around rocky outcroppings and evergreens. Cooper didn't risk stopping or looking back. Now they were truly on the run as they had never been.

He wanted to punch something. To kick himself, but he couldn't stop to take the time. Instead, he let the twigs, needles and branches that continually slapped him in the face punish him. He'd take it like a man. He deserved it, but he tried to shield Hadley from any thorns or branches as they ran.

They'd lingered too long in one place.

Cooper had scouted the area to within at least a square mile of the berm to see if the man after her had closed in on them by tracking them through the night. That would be the only way he could have covered that much ground.

"Give me the pack," he said through gasps.

"Why?"

"Just do it, but don't stop moving." Hadley let the pack slide off as she whipped past a tree.

Cooper urged her forward through the thick ferns and tree trunks. They had lost their lead.

Now. To get it back.

He continued jogging, pushing through the thick foliage as fast as possible, while he dug in the backpack. There. He yanked out the tracker.

"What are you doing?" Hadley glanced over her shoulder and tripped.

Cooper caught her, held her up and urged her forward. "Losing our tail. Wait here."

He ran in the opposite direction and then came back to her and they continued on. "I left it over there. Maybe that will lead him away from us."

"But I thought—"

Yeah, he'd been an idiot to think he could

somehow snag that assassin and make him talk. "Change of plans."

Add to that, he had the sick feeling that the man would continue to find them with or without that tracker. In fact, Cooper could almost wish for the cover of darkness at this moment. That would be an advantage to him. They had no choice but to make every effort to lose the assassin now and for good. Cooper had been arrogant, thinking he could draw the man to them and get the upper hand.

His overconfidence had almost gotten them killed.

Hadley stopped and bent over her thighs, gasping for breath. "What was that, Coop?"

"A rocket launcher."

"Are you kidding me? I rank rocket launcher status?"

"Evidently." Who was Hadley's father? Who was Hadley that someone would go to this much trouble to make sure she was killed? "But we need to keep going. We have to gain our lead back."

A skilled assassin like the one following them would likely be frustrated that he hadn't already killed Hadley and that she'd made him work his way through the wilderness—not everyone's cup of tea. Perhaps that was why the man had come loaded for bear, bringing a rocket launcher. On the other hand, maybe he considered this a thrill, a game.

"I hate to say this." Hadley slowed. "But I'm not sure I can run much farther. My side is hurting."

"Life or death, Hadley. Do you want to live?" And he'd done such a brilliant job helping her with that, taking her into the wilderness to hide and keep her safe. "But let's rest here."

She nodded, looking relieved.

"Never give up," he mumbled under his breath.

Guilt weighed on him, but he was in it now. No turning back. No handing her off to someone else. She deserved a better protector—but he was what she had. Hadley crouched down and rested against a tree trunk. Cooper watched and listened for their pursuer.

I can fight him again if I have to. I can lose him in this wilderness, too.

If only he wasn't out of ammo and hadn't lost his packs containing more. Excuses, excuses. He needed to listen to his own wilderness training advice—*focus on what you have, and don't waste time worrying about what you don't.*

But where was the assassin now?

By now, even if the man hadn't seen their escape he would be searching the debris for their bodies. When he failed to discover evidence he'd taken them out, he would search the woods next.

Hopefully he'd start by following the discarded tracker, but they couldn't count on that to throw him off their trail for long.

Cooper glanced down at Hadley—caught her watching him, her golden green eyes intense. She'd trusted him to get her to safety, but this hadn't gone down anything like he'd planned. He was no match for rocket launchers and since he was out of ammo, their best chance was to hide. It always came back to that and he was sick of constantly retreating. Like this enemy was one step ahead and outsmarted them at every turn.

He scraped a hand over his face and swiped away the sticks and dirt.

After another glance through the greenery, Cooper offered his hand to Hadley again and assisted her to her feet. He had an idea. He hoped this one would get them through. He pressed a finger to his lips and led Hadley away, hoping her assassin wasn't experienced at wilderness tracking. There was no time to cover their trail.

They reached the river again and Hadley looked up at him, a question in her eyes and not just a little fear. "No...no, I can't do that again. What are you thinking?"

They'd gained their lead and gotten ahead of the assassin by miles when the river took them away. It wasn't a bad idea to do so again. But, no... "We're not going to jump." He had a better idea.

* * *

The roar of the falls filled Hadley's ears, mist spraying her face.

Cooper edged closer.

What is he doing?

She would have asked, but that would mean yelling over the falls and they had to keep quiet.

Hadley struggled to follow Cooper as he climbed over boulders and trees and the gnarled roots that thrust from the edge. He was making his way to the waterfall. But why?

He glanced at her, then suddenly he disappeared behind the falls.

She blinked.

What just happened? Where had he gone? And was he just going to leave her standing out here?

Hadley didn't think she could follow him through that rushing wall, but then an arm reached through the curtain of water and grabbed her hand. Cooper tugged, wanting to pull her inside. Fear threaded through her belly as she blindly stepped into the unknown.

A cold rush doused her as she moved through until she stood beside Cooper. They were behind the waterfall in the cave created by falls eroding rock over time.

"How did you know this would be here?"

He grinned. "I didn't. That's why I had to check it out first."

"I thought this only happened in books and movies like *The Last of the Mohicans*." Heat crept up Hadley's neck. She wished she hadn't said her thoughts aloud. She certainly didn't want to imply that they were anything like those characters, who had fallen in love over the course of the story. "You're not going to leave me here, are you?"

The way Cooper studied her, the heat grew deeper in her cheeks. Maybe they were fighting for their lives, but they weren't in love.

To her surprise a slight grin crept into his lips. "No, but if I did, you know I would find you."

Had he read the book, too? Or just seen the movie? Did he love movies like that, the way she did? If so, that was something else they had in common. But she wouldn't bring that up. She shouldn't be thinking about it.

"Well, that's good to know." She fought the urge to smile. Somehow it didn't seem appropriate and she was embarrassed for bringing up such a passionate story. "Funny, the book was written by James Fenimore Cooper. His last name is the same as your first name."

He chuckled. "I'll be honest, that scene crossed my mind and it gave me the idea to look here."

What else was he thinking? An emotion she couldn't identify flickered behind his gaze. Her heart beat in an unfamiliar rhythm. Hadley could no longer hold his stare. Shivering, she hugged herself and looked away.

"Don't take this the wrong way." His voice was near, surprising her. Cooper's arms came around her and tugged her close.

Instantly, she was warm. She stiffened at first, then accepted the heat from his body and strength in his arms. "What are we doing here?"

"I think you know the answer."

"Hiding? Don't you think he'll look behind the waterfall? If he finds us, we're trapped." She glanced through the curtain of water—in patches she could make out the blurry world on the other side.

"I don't think he'll look here. But we can't travel fast enough to lose him if he's following our trail. And if he does look, I'll see him coming before he sees me."

"You're sure he won't use another rocket launcher?"

"Let's hope not. I doubt he would have carried more than one on his quest. Even one is a surprise."

"How long are we going to wait?"

"Just until I'm sure he's lost our tracks. I threw the tracker along an animal trail and we headed in the opposite direction remember? I'm hoping he'll think we dropped it or lost it but will continue along the path."

Hadley stepped away from him. Turned to face him. "And where are we headed, Coop?" Fear laced her voice, though she tried to hide it. "I don't see how this is ever going to end. Nothing I've planned has worked out for me. I tried to follow my father's instructions but it didn't work out. I couldn't get lost, disappear and get safe, even with your help."

By the look in his eyes, she knew he'd felt the sting of her words.

"I bear responsibility, Hadley. Nothing *I've* planned has worked out for us. I'll own up to that. But we can't give up."

Cooper kept his eyes on the blurry world beyond the falls. What was he thinking?

"Is there anything else you can tell me? Anything you haven't already told me?" He crossed his arms.

Acid churned in her stomach. "You know everything! If I knew something more, I would tell you! My life is at stake here, and now I've involved you."

"What was in the letter?"

"Wha—" Oh no, would he think she'd lied about it deliberately? She was going to tell him... eventually. "I'm sorry, I only just found the letter not long before you returned this morning. I read it then for the first time, I promise."

"I believe you—I saw that the envelope was still sealed. What did it say?"

Hadley crossed her arms now. The letter had been private from her father to her. It didn't feel right to just hand it over to Cooper for him to read for himself. She stared at the water worn, moss-covered rock floor beneath her feet. On the other hand, she owed him. He'd risked everything for her. Her angered subsided and she dropped her arms.

"I'm sorry for keeping it from you. You have a right to know. Everything's happening so fast and I—"

"It's all right, Hadley. I understand."

"When my father was bleeding to death, dying in my apartment, he told me to run. Hide. Not to trust anyone. That he'd given me everything I needed in the pack. I saw money and a passport and I've been running practically nonstop. I never dug deeper, looked further until today. In the letter, he gave me the name of someone to contact who can help hide me."

Cooper's forehead crinkled as he listened. "Okay, good. This is the way for you to be safe. We'll hike out of here. With that cash of yours, you can buy our way to the next town on the coast and get us out of the wilderness."

"Never thought I'd hear you say that. You're the wilderness guy."

She recalled the first time she'd met him, if you could call it that, when he'd sprung from nowhere and saved her from certain death. Cooper was an interesting combination of two parts wilderness, one part military background, if she'd pegged him right. He was a man who knew how to handle himself and she felt safe with him. She wouldn't have survived this long without him.

And there was more, much more about him that made her skin tingle and her thoughts turn to mush. Even now she breathed him in and it made her light-headed. She tried to shake it off, but it was nearly impossible with his proximity. When he stepped away from her, closer to the falls, she drew in a long, steadying breath. Better. That was better.

She'd never be able to truly, completely trust anyone when even the one person closest to her could live a lie, deceive her the way her father had. It was his job, and she understood, but it didn't matter. The wall had gone up around her heart. It wasn't coming down any time soon.

"What's the matter?" she asked.

"Nothing. Just thinking. This is good, Hadley. For the best. We head to the coast. That'll put some distance between us and the assassin. He's probably thinking since I'm the Wilderness, Inc., guy that I'll dig in and keep you here in this remote region because it's what I know. But even then, we have to be careful. We don't know if there are more assassins out there hunting you at the same time. Once you're on the coast, you can make contact with someone who can help you like your father arranged."

And just like that, she and Cooper would part ways. Hadley was surprised how much that thought bothered her. But then again, she didn't want to see him hurt because of her. She didn't want another person to die.

"I won't leave you until you're safe," he promised.

What if she was never safe again? What did that mean for Cooper? For either of them?

Cooper cleared his throat. She hadn't realized she was staring.

"Okay, I think we've waited long enough." He held out his hand. "You ready to go back out into the wild and dangerous world?

THIRTEEN

Exhausted, Hadley hiked behind Cooper. He knew the way, after all.

They'd exited the cave behind the waterfall on the other side of the river and headed west, toward the coast. He stopped in front of her, and she looked up to see a cabin rested through the trees, smoke rising from the chimney. What she wouldn't give to sit by a fire right now with a big cup of hot cocoa. "What are you going to do?"

"There's a couple of vehicles in the garage. Let's see if we can negotiate." He lowered his voice. "In a survival situation, we'd ask to use their phone, of course. Call the authorities. But with your state of affairs, we can't do that. And I'll need to use the cash your father gave you for a vehicle. Will that be all right?"

"Sure."

"Hand me a wad now. I don't want the guy living in that house to see how much is in the bag in case he gets some kind of idea."

"Why, do you know him? You don't trust him?"

"Russ Feldman used to live here with his wife, but moved out three year ago when she died. I don't know these people. They could help us or they could be trouble."

She thrust a few big bills in his hand. He jammed them in his pocket and started forward, then hesitated. "Oh, and stay behind me. Like I said, I'm not sure what to expect."

Hadley shrugged. Okay by her. He knew these reclusive wilderness types better than she did. Her hands in her jacket pocket, still cold and wet, she trudged behind him. The day had turned even colder. Maybe low fifties, high forties. Cooper clomped up the porch steps, making enough noise to scare the bears away and also to alert the household someone was at the door. Then he knocked.

Seconds ticked by.

No one answered.

Yet, there were vehicles in the garage—a truck and a motorcycle. They had a fire going. Clearly someone was home. Would it be too much to hope they would invite Hadley and Cooper inside to enjoy the fire and a bowl of stew? And then offer to take them to the nearest town? Hadley's gaze followed the rudimentary driveway—it disappeared through the trees. The private road could easily be miles. It would be nice to have some wheels at their disposal again.

He knocked again. "Sorry to disturb you but we need a little help."

Nothing.

Maybe they weren't in the house but nearby. Hadley stepped from the covered porch and searched the woods for a shed or garden. When she glanced back at the house, she saw the curtains move. "It's no use. They're not going to open the door."

He frowned. "We're willing to pay for your help."

After a few seconds he stepped back and eyed the windows. Frustration edged his jaw. Cooper shrugged and stepped off the porch. He headed away from the house along the drive.

Hadley hurried to keep up. "I don't get it. Why won't they help us?"

"Maybe it's a woman at home alone. She doesn't trust strangers."

"If so, then I don't blame her." Not anymore. "Maybe I should try."

"No."

She hiked next to him, keeping pace. "Why not?"

"Because I don't trust strangers, either."

"I'm tired, Coop. I don't want to whine, especially after you paid me such a compliment about not being a whiner. But I honestly don't think I can keep going like this." With the strain of the last two days, and especially the last few hours of hiking, her legs might collapse right out from under her at any moment.

Cooper stopped. Pointed at a thick-trunked conifer. "Wait over there, next to that tree."

"What are you going to do?"

"I'm going to be plenty generous, that's what. And when I get back, be ready."

Cooper didn't hike. He jogged up the winding trail of a driveway, or private road, then ducked back into the woods. She didn't like this at all. Why couldn't she go with him? Was it safe to stay here alone? She leaned against the tree and pressed deeper into a hollow of the trunk.

What if the assassin found her here by herself? Even with all her training, did she have the strength to fight him off until Cooper returned? All of those years, she'd never expected to actually have to use the skills that her father had taught her. But now she'd used them multiple times just in the past couple of days.

Just when it seemed Cooper had been gone much too long, pebbles crunched and twigs snapped.

Please, God, let it be Cooper. She peered around the tree.

It was him, pushing a motorcycle. Hadley

stepped out into the open. Crossed her arms. "You stole that! You can't do that."

"I paid for it, though."

"Does that matter if you took it without their permission?"

"I was more than generous. This is a Kawasaki KLR. Inexpensive adventure bike used for off roading. But it's good on pavement, too. Just not built for speed."

"I'm not interested in speed. Don't want to ride that, either, though it's better than walking. But just because it's inexpensive doesn't mean it's all right to take it."

"The point is I left them more cash than this is worth. They'll be able to replace it with a brand-new and better model. If they would have opened the door I could have explained this was life and death. I left them a note with the money."

She angled her head. "You did?"

"Yeah. Found a scrap of paper and a pencil on a work bench."

"What if the bike has some sort of sentimental value? Like it belongs to a son who's in the military. Or a deceased grandfather. No amount of money can replace that."

He gave her a silencing look. "You'd rather keep hiking?"

That was a tough question. "No."

"We can bring the bike back, once this is over, if it makes you feel any better."

"So do you think they know you took it?"

"I tried to push around the bushes and keep out of sight. No time to argue. But they'll know soon enough, if they don't already. Get on."

"Wait. No helmet?"

"Sorry. There wasn't one anywhere near the bike. If they have any, they just keep them inside, and that would have required breaking and entering. We're not that desperate yet. At least they left the keys in the ignition."

"Is this stuff you teach in your wilderness survival training?"

"Very funny."

Hadley climbed onto the back of the motorcycle.

"You need to grab on to me and hang on."

Slowly, she slid her arms around him. She shouldn't feel uncomfortable. This wouldn't be the first time she'd been this close to him. But each time she found herself next to him like this, her awareness of him grew.

He started the ignition, and the noise broke through the woods.

Yep. If the owners didn't know before, they knew now.

Cooper took off down the bumpy road too fast for comfort. He wasn't kidding—Hadley had to hang on or die. She squeezed her arms around him tighter and pressed her body against his back. The cold wind rushed over her. Hadley wanted to see where they were heading, watch the ride, but she would have needed goggles, a helmet, something to block the wind. Instead, she turned her face to the side and pressed it against Cooper's back. At least he was warm. Attractive, too, but that shouldn't matter.

If only she'd met Cooper under much different circumstances. But even if they had, then what? Her life was in the big city, where she had access to the kind of high society that would buy her art. His life was out here. No. They had to be forced together like this; otherwise their paths would never have crossed.

He'd gone out of his way to help her. For what reason, she couldn't know for certain. What she did know was that Cooper had structured his life around teaching people how to survive, so there was no way Cooper could turn his back on her. But something deeper drove him to risk everything, and Hadley wanted to know what it was. What pushed Cooper to put his life on the line for her? She had a feeling he'd hinted at it once before. She wanted to know Cooper.

And his secrets.

The motorcycle found the actual road and hit

pavement, jarring her. Cooper accelerated and took the mountain curves faster than Hadley wanted.

She prayed for safety.

The engine roared and the machine picked up even more speed, trees whipping by in a blur. Did he really have to go this fast? Hadn't he said this motorcycle, whatever it was called, wasn't built for speed?

Hadley had never been on a motorcycle before. If she could just forget that someone wanted her dead, she could imagine this as an adventure of a lifetime. But she couldn't forget, and she was hanging on quite literally for her life. She hated depending on others for her safety.

At least he seemed to be an all-around hero, and she was in good hands—until he handed her off to her father's contact. What did she really know about this man, Ronny Pager? Just that her father had given her the name. Until two days ago, her father had been her hero, but now she wasn't sure she could trust someone just on his word. She struggled to reconcile her confusing thoughts and jumbled emotions.

Cooper took a curve in the road and leaned accordingly, taking Hadley with him. Hadley's stomach tumbled. Nausea turned inside, but it wasn't from the bike ride.

Her father...

He'd worked for the CIA. He'd said this could

be about revenge. An operation he was involved with in the past. And like the man who killed him, and the man who was trying to kill her, had her father been an assassin, too?

Cooper realized he was pushing the speed on the bike, scaring Hadley, but he'd seen a vehicle behind them rounding a corner just as he'd steered onto the road.

Maybe it was nothing, but he wouldn't take any chances. They would be at Gold Beach in fifteen minutes, less if he kicked up the speed.

There was that car again. Not so unusual on the one road between Gideon and Gold Beach—but the car sped up to approach them.

He felt Hadley's arms tighten as she pressed into him. Good. He pushed the bike and, unfortunately, was rewarded with the car coming up directly behind them, pacing them. He feared driving any faster, imperiling their lives more than they already were.

Why couldn't they catch a break?

How much was the contract on Hadley? Why was her death this important? Too many questions when he needed to focus on one thing.

The road.

The car behind—an old Chevy Nova—tried to catch him. He hoped it wasn't a souped-up classic. If he could trust the paint, the Nova was an old clunker. If the car caught up to him, would the driver ram them, destabilizing the bike and sending Cooper and Hadley flying? Or was Cooper beyond paranoid to think the car was after them? Had the assassin done the same as they had—taken the next ride he could find, and in this case, a Chevy Nova?

He could expect dangerous twists and turns the next five miles, in which he'd have to slow the bike. But then the driver behind them would have to slow, too.

Then Cooper saw his chance.

Up ahead he was closing in on another vehicle heading west as well as a truck headed toward them from the opposite direction.

In his mirror, the Nova inched closer, coming faster.

Close enough now, Cooper could see the driver's face. The driver was the assassin from the shop. He'd recognize that face anywhere.

Cooper took the chance when the road straightened before the next twist—he accelerated, speeding around the car in front and passing it.

Hadley yelled his name into his back. But he focused on the road. The oncoming grill of a truck. The truck driver's horn blared as Cooper whipped the motorcycle back around and pressed forward.

Now, the twists in the road would make passing nearly impossible.

He had four miles to escape. The assassin couldn't pass the car that was between them without risking his own life. But was that enough of a guarantee? Anyone who killed people for a living feared nothing. Valued nothing. Even his own life. Cooper didn't slow his speed, even when he couldn't see any vehicles behind him.

He pushed the bike even as the gas tank neared empty. He could make two miles on fumes.

"Cooper!" Hadley had shifted behind him.

She wanted his attention, but he couldn't give it. Not yet.

"Just a little more." He threw the words over his shoulder but couldn't be sure she heard him over the bike and the wind.

She had no choice but to hang on for the ride.

Finally, the road neared the estuary where the Rogue River met the Pacific Ocean in Gold Beach. Cooper turned south on Highway 101 and crossed the bridge, then pushed toward town. Hadley loosened her grip if only a little.

Hold on.

He knew she needed a break. They'd lost their tail for now, but it wouldn't be hard for the man to find them again. The road emptied out in one place, and there were only two directions to go. Cooper would try to stay lost in the small town, for the moment.

Just beyond Gold Beach, he pulled over onto

a side road that led to the beach. He steered the bike as far as he could until he had to park, but at least they were right up on the beach.

When he stopped the bike, Hadley was the first off. She stumbled forward and ran toward the waves, her hands gripping her midriff. The beach was cold and windy most of the time, and nothing at all like the southern California coast.

But it had a beauty all its own.

Just like Hadley.

There were clusters of rocks jutting out of the sand and ocean, some as big as islands, dotting the shoreline. If you timed it right, tide pools showcased brilliantly colored starfish and anemones. Cooper wished he could walk the beach with Hadley under entirely different circumstances.

He slid from the bike and caught up with her. "You okay?"

"What do you think?"

"Sorry about that. But he was behind us and…"

A huge breaker hit the rocks nearest them, and the crashing roar drowned out anything else he might have said.

"No, Coop. You don't need to apologize. You're helping me. You've saved my life a dozen times over by now. And I don't know why." She looked up at him, her green eyes brilliant like emeralds filled with golden sparkles, and her strawberry-blond hair whipped into a frenzy from the ride, framing her face just so.

Something deep inside shifted—on a tectonic scale—and stirred up a familiar, steady rhythm. One he best forget.

"Why are you helping me?" Desperation edged her voice.

She wanted to know that *now*? What had set her off?

"I've already told you. Helping people is…what I do." Though he could see in her eyes that she knew it went much deeper than that, hence her question.

Admittedly, he'd never had to go this far, this extreme, before—except as a Green Beret. Helping Hadley was the right thing to do and he'd had no choice. But more than that—what she was really asking—he wasn't ready to share with her. He wasn't sure he ever would.

But he did know that this time, this chance he had to help someone as desperate as Hadley, he had to succeed. He'd take it all the way. He'd like to set things right if he could, stay by her side until he could make sure the threat to her safety was identified. But it looked like the issue of her safety had been taken from his hands.

Maybe once she was safely away, he could work on figuring out the person behind the contract from his end. No one should have to live a life looking over their shoulders.

Squinting against the wind, she took in the rocky outcroppings, the sea spray when breakers hit the rocks. The rock-laden beach went on and on—the Oregon coast was one of the most beautiful in the world. Again, Cooper wished he could walk it with her when this was over. The continued unbidden thoughts surprised him. He could have no future with her.

She glanced at him. "We should call the name on the letter. Find out what I'm supposed to do and then you can get back to your life."

At least since there was someone else out there to help her, and Cooper could release her into this person's hands. Then he wouldn't have to reach out to his connection. He shook his head, hating that his mind had gone there.

A strange sensation blew over him—he wasn't sure he could get back to his life. Not without Hadley. But she sounded more than ready to be rid of him.

Who could blame her?

FOURTEEN

Hadley once again straddled the motorcycle, her arms around Cooper, holding on as they went in search of a phone. He'd stopped to get fuel already, yet though they'd hoped to find a phone booth at the station, they were disappointed. Pay phones weren't so easy to find these days, nor were there any emergency call boxes along the road.

At least the gas station had snacks and they guzzled sodas and candy bars for energy, and then kept moving. Cooper headed farther up the road and out of town, hoping to put more distance between them and the assassin. Maybe changing vehicles would help, too. She had to stay alive long enough to make contact with the man her father had said could help her disappear.

Miles of ocean passed by on their right, jagged, steep rocks called sea stacks thrust out of the shoreline until civilization once again encroached in the form of a small coastal town. He slowed the motorcycle and turned into the parking lot for a shopping strip and then into an alley out of view. Hadley got off the motorcycle with Cooper.

He glanced around them and started walking. "Let's try to stay out of the open and keep a sharp eye."

"You think he'll find us?"

"Eventually, yes. But this time he doesn't have the GPS tracker to rely on, so it will take him longer."

Hadley shook her head. She didn't understand, but she hadn't majored in tracking people and killing them.

"We can get some grub here and a couple of cheap phones to make our calls. The sooner we can get you into this Ronny Pager's hands and away from those who would kill you, the better."

Before they stepped from behind the alley, Cooper stopped her. Pressed his hand against her shoulder. "I've done the best I could, Hadley. I just wish it had been enough. I'm glad there are options and your father planned for the worst-case scenario."

Yes, her father had been prepared for her to need to change her identity and disappear. Hadley still couldn't believe it. And yet at the same time, the letter said that he expected her to follow her dreams. The two goals were diametrically opposed.

Cooper stared at her, expecting a reply. "It was enough, Coop. You've gotten me this far. And I can never repay you."

"No need for that. But if you survive and make a life for yourself, that will be enough."

Again, something in his voice, something about him conveyed he was driven to prove something to himself. She wanted to know what that was. But she had no right to pry in his personal business—not if he didn't want her to know. They weren't friends, not really. She was just a complication that had dropped into his life and messed everything up for a few days. The sooner she could make that call, the sooner they could both be safe.

She nodded and they exited the alley to walk the outdoor strip mall. At the far end was a small sandwich shop and a dollar discount store. Across from that, a convenience store.

If she bought a burner phone, she'd still have to charge it before she could use it. That would take hours.

Seeming to read her thoughts, Cooper gestured to the phone booth on the corner.

Relief rushed through her. Maybe things were beginning to go their way for once.

"I don't have any change," she said.

To her surprise Cooper chuckled. "Let's fuel up first. That candy bar from the gas station only made me hungrier. I don't know about you, but

I could use something substantial." He opened the door to the submarine sandwich shop, letting Hadley go through first. "Pay cash and we can get change."

"Fine, but let's get them to go." Though eager to reach the contact, Hadley found herself wishing she could sit at a table and have a relaxed lunch with Cooper like a normal couple.

Couple?

They ordered their sandwiches, paid and received change, grabbed their bags and drinks and exited the sandwich shop. By the time they reached the phone booth, Cooper had already downed half his sandwich. Hadley was a close second. She hadn't realized how hungry she was, even though she'd eaten a small snack.

Standing at the booth, she glanced up at him and drank tea from her straw. Cooper's steel-blue eyes suddenly turned warm as they glanced over her face and lingered on her lips, then a grin tugged the edges of his mouth.

"You've got something." He pointed to a place just above his own lip.

Hadley tried to wipe her face, but apparently missed. He took a napkin and wiped the spot away for her.

"It seems you're always cleaning up my messes."

"Indeed."

And that would be ending soon, when she met

up with this new contact, whoever he was. The way Cooper looked at her now, a kind of sadness in his eyes, she had a feeling he was thinking the same thing. But why wouldn't he want to be rid of her? Why wouldn't he want to be free of this situation?

He handed off the coins. Hadley pulled the letter from the bag.

The letter shook in her hands. "Well, I guess this is it."

Moisture slicked her palms. Why was she this nervous? Terrified even?

"It's going to be okay, Hadley. Remember, I'm with you until you're safe somewhere." His words bolstered her.

Glancing at him, she searched his eyes, his face, trying to decide if there was a hidden meaning behind his words. Was he insinuating that this contact might not be safe for Hadley? She hadn't considered that.

She put the coins in the slot and punched in the number, then handed the letter off to Cooper. The phone pressed against her ear, she listened as it rang several times. With each ring, her anxiety ratcheted up. What if she got no answer? Then what would she do?

"Hello?" a man answered.

"Yes, This is…" What name should she give?

She hadn't thought that far, or if she should even give her name.

"Hello?"

"Yes, I'm calling for Ronny Pager."

"What's this about?"

Why hadn't her father given her more information?

"I… I was given his name by a friend and told to contact him."

"Ronny is a woman."

"Okay, well, it's important that I speak with her."

"She's gone."

"Can you give her a message for me?" Hadley's voice trembled. She wasn't sure what her message should be. She didn't have a phone yet so the woman couldn't call her back. Why did this have to be so hard?

"You don't understand… She's dead. She was murdered. Who is this again?"

Cooper wished he could hear what the person on the other end of the phone was saying. He definitely didn't like Hadley's expression—a look of shock and confusion.

As she slowly replaced the receiver, just before she ended the call, he could hear a man demanding to know her name.

"What happened?"

Hadley stared at the concrete.

"Hadley, what is it?"

Finally, she peered up at him. "She's dead."

Not good. Not good at all. "Did they say what happened?"

"She was murdered." She pressed her face into her hands. "I didn't ask when or how."

Cooper wrapped his arms around her, wanting to shelter her from all that was wrong in the world. Sounded like all the "loose" ends were being tied up, all right. Except for Hadley. But saying the words out loud wouldn't change things, and he didn't want to scare her any more than she already was. He didn't want to admit that he was scared, too. But anger and determination quickly replaced his fear.

"Let's go, then." Cooper ushered her forward and back to the alley with their motorcycle, though he knew they should try to get a different vehicle.

"Where, Cooper? Where can we possibly go now?"

"It's on to Plan C."

"Right. Because Plan A and B didn't work. Just what is Plan C, Cooper?"

He rubbed a hand over his jaw, unsure if he liked the accusation in her tone. Maybe the truth was too hard to face—he couldn't give Hadley what she needed. Cooper waited for Hadley to climb onto the bike before he answered her question.

"First, we're going to get out of here. Get a good lead on the assassin. Then I'm going to contact someone who can help. I didn't want to go there, but I see now, there is no other way."

"Tell me what happened to you, Cooper? What happened in your past that was so bad?"

Well, it was now or never. Might as well tell her everything. He glanced down the alley in both directions, making sure they were still safely hidden and alone.

"My father insisted we all go into the military for our training to be in wilderness survival business. He runs a wilderness survival training facility near Portland that trains various branches of the US Military—Special Forces and elite units—along with law enforcement, search and rescue, anyone who wants special training. He was all about the business and we were expected to participate. My younger brother Jeremy had different dreams. He didn't like violence or blood and just wanted to…he wanted to paint.

"Paint?"

"He was an artist like you." Cooper watched her reaction and knew it was right to share this with her, no matter how painful it was to him. "He didn't want to go into the service, but he went because my father can be very persuasive.

Did one tour. Between the four of us—Alice, Gray, me and Jeremy—he and I were the closest. I tried to watch out for him as best I could. But the military didn't make him stronger, it sucked him dry. Sucked all the life out of him. When he came home he suffered with PTSD. I watched him spiral downward, but he never got help because he didn't want to appear weak to our father. I tried to help, but I wasn't enough. I couldn't stop it." Cooper tried to restrain the anguish in his voice, but by Hadley's expression, he knew he'd failed.

She pressed a hand on his arm. "Coop, what happened?"

"I watched him jump from a cliff. I tried to save him. I rushed there, hoping I'd make it in time. That I could talk him down. But I couldn't stop him." Cooper's stared at the garbage in the alley. "He killed himself."

Reliving the moment punched him in the gut.

"My father blamed me for not being able to stop it. For not trying hard enough to help Jeremy be strong. For not watching out for him. I blame myself, too." He wanted to look away, but the compassion he saw in her eyes held him captive. And everything he'd tried to ignore became clear—he was beginning to care about her in a deeper way. And that was terrifying because he feared he wouldn't be able to save her, either.

"Is that why *you* train people in wilderness survival?"

Her question surprised him. He'd already explained it was a family thing, though he'd branched off into his own wilderness training business apart from his father. "What do you mean?"

"The way you put your heart into things, I get the feeling you teach others to survive in a physical way because you couldn't be there for your brother, to help him survive his emotional and mental issues. And now…that's why you've put everything into helping me. You think you can maybe redeem yourself."

He shrugged. Averted his gaze. Hadley had seen beyond the obvious. Seen too much and he didn't like to be psychoanalyzed. And now, too late, he wished he hadn't told her anything.

"You can't blame yourself for your brother's decisions or your father's reactions. But who am I to tell you that? You don't know me that well."

She didn't understand the half of it. "I wanted you to know this, so you'd know the kind of person who is helping you now." Someone who failed to save a life—one of the most important lives to him personally.

Looking down at the motorcycle beneath her, she appeared to contemplate his words. That was fair—he'd given her a lot to think about.

Doubts hammered away at his confidence. And

yet, Hadley had no one else. He'd already decided he would see this through. He took her hand in his, willing her to understand. "Despite all that, I won't let anything happen to you, Hadley. I won't let him kill you."

He couldn't watch her die. He had to be enough this time. *God, please, let it be so.*

"I understand why you're so determined to help me now, but Cooper, what did you do in the military? I mean, have you ever killed anyone?"

Seriously?

"I was in in Special Forces in the army. A Green Beret. Yes, Hadley, I've killed before. More than that, I can't tell you. They were mostly covert operations, of course. I would have stayed in the service, but my family needed me. My brother needed me. And I lost him anyway."

The wind kicked up, blowing papers through the alley. He was blind sitting in here. They should get going. He blew out a breath, climbed on and started the motorcycle. Once Hadley had placed her arms around him nice and tight, he took them back out on the road again.

Guilt lashed at him. She was depending on him, and with her life on the line, it seemed increasingly obvious she had the wrong guy.

FIFTEEN

Hadley held tightly to Cooper once again.

His confession remained lodged in her heart and mind. Saving her was personal to him. Now she understood what had driven him to help her. Yet what did the reasons matter? It was his actions that counted. They had been thrown together in this fight for survival and without him, she wouldn't be alive. She couldn't fight a skilled assassin off by herself forever.

She owed this man. Big-time. But she was beginning to fear his choices, his courses of action. All of their plans seemed to fall apart within a few hours. They were on the defensive at every turn.

The assassin continued to have the upper hand.

Cooper steered through a curve in the road and Hadley held on tighter. She liked the feel of his strong back and arms, and in a short time, her emotions were latching on to him, not even counting her attraction to the guy. Who wouldn't be attracted to this rugged wilderness hero. He was strong and capable and fought for the innocent. He had his flaws, sure, but didn't everyone?

Except, not everyone had killed someone. Cooper had killed. The thought of it scared her a little, even though she knew she was being unfair, giving that he'd acted in the line of duty—just like her father probably had. That was the real problem—Cooper had secrets just like her father had. Secrets he could never share. She couldn't let herself get any deeper with Cooper. It was just too dangerous to trust, especially someone with Cooper's background. Covert operations in Special Forces. Her father had played a part in a covert mission that had cost him his life. Hadley's world had been shaken because of her father's secret. Whether or not she survived remained to be seen. But she wouldn't let things get personal between her and Cooper.

The way the cold wind whipped around her, Hadley was grateful she could use his back as a protective shield. She squeezed her eyes shut, tears sliding from the corners. If only she didn't have to hold on to him like this. Count on him like this. What if he failed her like he'd failed his brother?

But that was different, she told herself. Her brother had wanted to die—how could Cooper save him from his own decisions?

In that moment when he'd shared about his past, she'd seen the pain in his eyes. She understood the pain—she carried a similar ache over her mother who'd died while giving birth to Hadley, though she had no control over that. Over her father who'd died while trying to save her.

No matter how far she ran, she could never escape the truth. People died because of her, loved ones and even sometimes people she barely knew, like the cabdriver who'd been shot just for giving her a ride.

Suddenly Cooper accelerated and maneuvered—more like swiveled—between cars on the two-lane highway that skirted the coast. She squeezed him hard. What was he doing?

Then…she *knew*.

She twisted her head to get a glimpse behind her.

Another motorcycle was closing in on them and fast.

Oh, Lord, no!

Hadley couldn't take much more of this, especially from the back of a motorcycle. They hugged a rocky cliff face, which flew by in a speedy blur. Vehicles honked when they passed too close, too reckless.

"Cooper!" She didn't want to distract him, but neither did she want to die on this road.

Between the motorcycle's roar and the wind

gusting through her hair and ears, she had no idea if he heard her, or if he even responded until he tensed against her. She hadn't thought his muscles could be any more taut.

Hadley risked another glimpse behind. The other motorcycle was gaining on them. What would the man do once he was close enough? Ram into them? Risk tumbling to his death on his own motorcycle?

But she got her answer soon enough.

Keeping one hand on the handlebars, he slipped the other into his jacket and pulled out a weapon.

Attuned to listening to Hadley despite the noise, he heard her frantic call, heard the desperation in her voice and knew they were in trouble. He glanced in the mirror.

Yep. Out of time.

He pressed forward in the seat and swerved the bike to the side, going around the car in front of him on the shoulder.

Hadley was going to die one way or another if he didn't get her off this road. But then, with an assassin on their tail, it would be a fight to the death.

Who would win?

Cooper zipped around the car, hearing the blare of the horn loudly, but the car also swerved to the left, giving him more room, and cutting off the assassin who tried to follow him. Cooper leaned deeper, but this bike just wasn't built for this type of speed.

He punched it anyway.

The road grew steeper, straining the motorcycle's engine, and the bike slowed.

Come on, come on, come on...

If he could just put some distance between them and this man set on killing Hadley.

His gut ached from the tension. Hadn't that been what he'd tried to do from the start—give them some space, some time to put protections in place? Yet nothing he tried seemed to work. Even getting rid of the tracking device hadn't kept them from being followed. He steered around another curve in the road and just as the road dipped, he spotted a turnout with a trail. Cooper took it, the bike jolting from the change in the road. He had to slow the machine to manage the gravel path but pushed the bike harder once he got his bearings. Like Rooster Cogburn in *True Grit*, he was killing the beast beneath him to save the girl.

The road turned into dirt and rock, but he accelerated. Had the assassin followed?

A glance in the mirror told him yes.

Good.

They were playing for keeps.

Though his initial intention had been to lose the man and regroup, he doubted it would do any good. Sooner or later, they would have to face this man down. Might as well get it over with. It was now or never. He would fight the man here and get the upper hand so they could find out who had put the contract on Hadley and end it. Cooper had to win this. There could be no other outcome.

He pushed the bike harder until he neared the top of the hill overlooking the rocky Oregon coast and miles and miles of the Pacific Ocean. He skidded to a stop, careful not to drop the bike on them.

"Get off, Hadley. Run and hide."

"What?" Her eyes were wide as she climbed from the vehicle.

"We have only seconds to take cover." He didn't have time to explain his plan as he dragged her behind him through the trees and around a large pile of boulders. "Hide in here. I'm going to take care of this once and for all."

"But Cooper!" She pulled him back. "You don't have a gun. You can't fight him without a weapon. This wasn't how we were supposed to take him down. Remember, Coop, we were going to draw him to us *after* we made a plan."

"We're never going to be far enough ahead, Hadley." And the truth of that reflected in her disappointed eyes.

Something deep inside stirred. Maybe he shouldn't have, but Cooper tugged Hadley to him and kissed her hard. He released her just as abruptly. "Just in case. Now, hide and don't come out. No matter what."

He left her standing there with her eyes wide.

"You're crazy, you know that?" she mumbled behind him.

"Yeah," he mumbled under his own breath. If he was about to face certain death—well, hopefully his death wasn't completely certain—he'd wanted to kiss her just once.

Though it had been fast and quick, he'd felt the tension in her, the attraction. And he could almost grin at that except he heard the other motorcycle stop a few yards away and out of sight.

Cooper hunkered down and crept behind rocks and trees. He had to be the first to attack. Surprise the guy and take the weapon. But catching him off guard wouldn't be easy. The man had to know that his approach hadn't gone unnoticed. Pressed behind the thick trunk of a cedar, Cooper peeked around the bark, eyeing the rock and dirt trail, boulders and trees.

Listening, he heard nothing at all.

Was the guy sneaking around from the other side? Was Hadley in danger where he'd left her?

Cooper had to think like this man. What would he do if he were an assassin on this same mission?

Reconnaissance.

Which is what Cooper himself was doing. He wished he hadn't left Hadley alone.

A scream resounded through the woods.

Hadley!

Cooper raced to where he'd left her, careful he didn't inadvertently draw fire from the assassin. Branches and needles scratched his cheeks as he ran through the woods, trying to keep it quiet. When he made the place where Hadley should have been, she was gone. Cooper didn't dare call out her name. Where could she have gone?

Did the assassin have her?

Panic raked over him. He tried to breathe.

Had the man pushed Hadley over? Cooper risked a glimpse over the ledge.

God, please, no, no, no...

Nausea swirled.

Waves crashed against rocks, but just beneath the cliff's edge, he caught sight of someone making their way along a terraced ledge below.

SIXTEEN

Hadley plastered her body against the rough, cutting edges of the rocky ledge.

This man was ruthless in tracking them. He would follow Hadley to the end of the earth and kill her. And not just her, he'd kill Cooper, too. What were they going to do?

She'd moved just as a bullet whizzed by and ricocheted off a rock. When she'd first seen the assassin making his way around toward where she'd hidden, Hadley had screamed and fled, hoping Cooper had heard her and would know where the assassin had gone. She'd had no choice but to flee her hiding place and climb down onto the ledge.

Where else could I go?

Pushing her way along the sea cliff wall, she could hear the ocean waves crashing a hundred feet below. She hoped to find some way to crawl back up to safety on the other side of this ledge, but fear strangled her, shutting down her coherent thoughts. What happened to the girl her father had taught to defend herself? Had she died with her father?

The sun descended slowly, moving toward the horizon as marine fog rolled in from the southwest. Breathtaking beauty brought tears to her eyes. She wanted to live to see another day. She wanted to survive to enjoy the splendor of creation like never before. Even as an artist, nature had never moved her like it did at this moment when she was so close to facing her own mortality. It was bittersweet.

God, I don't want to die. Help me. Help Cooper. Keep him safe.

Just two days ago she had taken her life for granted. Taken God for granted, that He listened to what few prayers she sent His way. She hadn't seriously needed Him all that much. She saw that now. And now she needed Him like never before.

Her heart hammered her rib cage.

This was it. This had to be it. She was going to die. *God...*

But she had to try. *Never give up.*

She'd heard Cooper mumble the words. Her father had said them, too, only differently. Never give up your dreams.

If Hadley was about to die, she would die fighting.

Seeing no way to climb up where the ledge

ended, Hadley pressed into a crevice to hide. Had the assassin seen where she'd gone? Would he follow her?

If so, then coming here had been suicide. She was trapped.

Cold and wet, the wind gusts pierced her like icy needles. She wanted this day to be over.

Just end already.

She almost didn't care how it ended.

Then she saw him.

The assassin. He'd shoved his black sunglasses over his head as he slowly crept along the ledge, gripping his weapon. So Cooper hadn't found him first, then. Her spirits sagged. Disappointment lodged in her throat.

God, help me. What am I supposed to do now?

He was coming.

He would find her soon.

It was up to her. She couldn't fight him when he held a weapon. She couldn't compete with that. There was only one thing she could do.

Hadley stepped out where he could see her. He pointed his gun at her.

Quickly, she said, "It's one thing to win with a weapon, but can you win in hand-to-hand combat?"

His grin curled into a snarl, but he said nothing at all. He put his weapon down a few feet away. Held his hands up and waved her away from the ledge. This would be a precarious fighting position. Did he know what had happened to his predecessor? Didn't he have a little fear?

She positioned herself to fight him, and they faced each other, pacing in a semicircle. Cognizant of the hundred-foot drop, Hadley tried to remain with the cliffside to her back. Then it started.

She fought for her life, knowing that to keep it, she would likely have to kill this man. Kill another human being.

And Hadley wasn't sure she had it in her.

Never give up...

He was strong, so strong. Hadley focused on one thing—the fight. She let herself fall into the almost zen-like state of pure instinct and reflex earned from hours and hours of practice. Just like her father had taught her, she gave into the flow of Krav Maga. Somehow she had to take control of the situation. But too many hours of living on the run weighed on her.

She must get the weapon he'd set down. But how?

Cooper appeared in her peripheral vision. He stumbled, a bit. Was he injured? Shot? That must be it. The other man saw him, too, and faster than she could have imagined, the assassin grabbed his weapon from where it lay a few feet away. His intentions were clear, but Hadley kicked the weapon from his grasp before he could shoot Cooper. She received a punch right to her face for her efforts. She fell back against the rock wall and caught her breath as pain shot through her back. But she was alive, and grateful Cooper was still alive, too, and that he'd shown up when he had.

But how to keep them that way?

The assassin fought Cooper now.

Her vision still blurred from the blow she'd received, she blinked a few times trying to see clearly. Because he was sluggish and possibly injured, Cooper wasn't on the winning side of the fight. Cooper was going to die if Hadley didn't do something.

Where was the weapon she'd kicked away? She scrambled, trying to avoid the men as they fought, searching for the discarded gun. When she glanced back at Cooper, he stood at the edge of the cliff.

The assassin held another gun at his head.

Cooper stared down the muzzle of the weapon. *So this is the end.* *I failed!* *I failed Hadley. I failed everyone!*

What if he just fell backward, and dropped into the ocean? It would be a fitting end, considering his brother's death. Cooper deserved to die like that, didn't he?

A cell phone rang.

Cooper startled.

The assassin frowned and whipped out his phone, cursing at the timing of the call.

To Cooper's surprise the man answered. Another string of curses. "Your timing couldn't be worse. Yes, yes, it's almost done. I'll call you back." He ended the call.

"This was supposed to be a simple job. You have caused me more trouble than I could have thought possible. There's nothing I hate worse than roughing it. Camping. I'm no different than you. Served time in the military and hated every minute. So there's nothing I'd like more than to make you suffer before I end this and collect my cash. I think I'll take the cash in her pack, too, just as a bonus, even though someone wants that back. But before you die, know that I'm going to have some fun with her before I kill her. You can suffer with that certainty for the next few seconds before I kill *you*."

A deep shuddering sigh passed through Cooper. The man's words sickened him.

"Who is behind this?" If Cooper was about to die, he wanted to know. "At least tell me, tell her, what this is all about." *Before you kill us.*

But Cooper couldn't say the words.

"Funny thing, that. I don't know who it is, so I can't tell you. It's a voice and a number, but no face or name. I would say it's nothing personal, but that has changed."

There had to be something he could do. But no, he had to admit to himself he'd failed. There was nothing more to be done.

Gunfire resounded, echoing against the sea cliff and dying away as waves buffeted the rocks below.

Cooper waited for the pain to slam him. For darkness to take him.

Instead, confusion, then dawning realization crept into the assassin's gaze.

He released his weapon and the cell phone, then he stumbled to the side and tumbled over the cliff, his body dropping to the ocean below and into the rocks. A wave crashed over the out-croppings and then the body was gone, dragged under and out to sea.

Hadley stood there, weapon in hand, eyes and mouth open wide as though in shock.

Heart pounding, Cooper fell to his knees. She'd saved him. Hadley had killed the assassin and saved Cooper. Saved them both. She let the gun fall from her hands.

"Oh, Cooper!" Hadley ran to him and met him on the ground, hugging him. She sobbed against him, and he almost joined her.

Instead, he held her to him, pressed his hand around her neck, his other arm around her waist.

She had to be suffering from many things right now, including the terrible weight of knowing she'd just killed a man. He needed to reassure her and spoke into her ear. "Hadley, thank you. You saved my life."

Cooper struggled to comprehend how things had gone down just now, and he hated to think that if it hadn't been for her own courage and strength, Hadley would have died. He would have let her down again. But he couldn't think like that. This was far from over, and she needed him to be strong, not drowning in guilt.

He focused on Hadley for now. Her softness pressed against him, and as he comforted her—as they comforted each other—her sobs finally subsided.

"You're going to be okay." He didn't bring up the dead guy. Didn't want to mention him.

Then she giggled.

Had she snapped? Maybe he'd spoken too soon. Cooper eased back so he could look her in the eyes. The sun was quickly setting—a spectacular sight on the Pacific. But Cooper only had eyes for Hadley.

"Hadley? You okay?"

"Yes. This has driven me crazy, I guess. But I was just thinking that if this happens again, we can just draw the bad guy to a cliff somewhere. We have a good track record with cliffs."

Yeah. She was in shock. Though he supposed she had a point. He crinkled his brow, wanting to laugh with her at her twisted sense of humor. It was fitting, after all. But he couldn't. "The last guy who died said another would come for you. So until we find out who is behind this, it's not over."

Her smile faded. She hiccupped. "I know, I just...well, the cliff. We'll just wait for him here."

Cooper wanted to kiss her again, like he'd done before, but that was then and this was now. He wasn't the guy for her. "No. I have a better idea."

"A Plan D?"

"No. Still Plan C." Cooper picked up the assassin's cell phone. "The last call on this phone, Hadley, the last incoming call might give us some answers. I don't want to mess with evidence, but we're desperate and I need a phone. I need to call a guy who can help us find those answers." The man he should have called long ago. "I'm going to call someone who can help. Someone with the connections you need to end this."

"I don't know, Cooper. Are you sure you can trust this person?" Real fear, real desperation lodged in her gaze along with a transparency he hadn't seen in her before.

And he saw it clear enough now. She was losing confidence in him.

His fault.

All his fault.

He had to remedy that.

Cooper stared at the phone. He was tempted to check the number for the last call the assassin had received—that call might identify the person they were after—but only if he gave this phone to the right people. Those in the know. He punched in the number, torn between hoping it would go to voice mail, and understanding he needed the man to answer and now. He closed his eyes, dreading the moment he would hear the older voice, and knowing it was the only way.

She grabbed his arm to pull the phone away. "Who, Cooper? Who are you calling?"

"Ethan Wilde. My father."

SEVENTEEN

Stay here.

Cooper had told her to wait for him. More like commanded.

There was nothing she hated worse than being told what to do. Well, maybe she hated waiting more. The fact she had to wait here in this lonely, dank room didn't make it any easier.

Hadley paced in the motel room—the best Cooper could find in the small coastal town. She'd never explored the Oregon Coast like this before and hadn't realized how many of these small towns dotted the coast.

She wasn't sure if that was good or bad. Would she and Cooper be easier to find this way? It wouldn't be easy for someone tracking them to guess which town they'd chosen. But on the other hand, they were bound to stand out to the locals. Better to hide in the wilderness again or a big city than a small town along the sparse Oregon coast. But how did she convince him?

His dad had told them to go to a motel and wait there, that someone would come for them.

Right.

Cooper was dead set on waiting because a man he hadn't spoken to in years told him to.

Maybe she shouldn't complain—she had survived. Again. And she was tucked away from the elements in a warm room instead of racing to her death on a wild motorcycle ride in the cold.

Though the motel was situated on the ocean side of Main Street and Hadley's room faced the west, only darkness stared back from the windows. She couldn't watch the ocean but heard the waves crashing against the rocky shore along with the wind whipping against the walls of the building. Both seemed to scream—"Leave now. Leave before it's too late."

And that echoed in her head reminding her of her father's warning.

Leave now before he finds you and kills you. Trust no one.

Hadley smashed a pillow over her face and screamed into it.

Who? Who wants to kill me?

She contemplated her father's instructions.

What if she just started over? She knew more about what to expect, what she was dealing with this time. What if she tried again on her own?

She had her cash. She didn't have transportation, but she could buy something. Follow Cooper's lead and offer cash for a quick and convenient getaway vehicle.

Cooper had gone to grab them fast food. She could be gone before he got back.

Was she crazy to sit here and wait for him? How could she trust anyone, especially Cooper's father? How could Cooper even trust his father, a man he hadn't talked to in years?

God, what do I do?

And she'd killed a man.

Her hands trembled. Hadley stopped pacing to look at her hands. Her artist's hands had held a gun, pulled the trigger. The images accosted her again and again. A recurring nightmare, only she was awake.

Stop it! Stop thinking about that.

She'd had no choice.

It was either that or watch him shoot Cooper and then turn on her.

Cooper would die before this was over if she didn't break away from him. Maybe she would, too, but better she took no one else with her.

Maybe she should leave Cooper here and disappear on her own. There might not be a better opportunity for her to escape. Without the tracker, she would have a better chance, especially if she was alone and kept well hidden.

Cooper would be angry, and she could imagine his steely-blue eyes that had warmed for her turning cold again because she hadn't trusted him. That would hurt him beyond words. They'd crossed a line somewhere along the way and she cared about Cooper in a way she shouldn't. And yeah, wanting to get away from him was more about him getting hurt, him dying because of her, than her lack of ability to trust him. But she wouldn't stick around long enough to try and explain that.

She couldn't go through this anymore. Couldn't watch him die, too, just like her father. Hadley snatched her backpack and slipped it on. She closed her eyes and imagined the surprise in his when he found her gone. Why did she have to torture herself?

Hadley sighed and dropped the bag to the floor. She should at least leave Cooper a note to tell him she appreciated his help.

Why, Cooper? Why do you trust your father this much?

Footsteps resounded from outside through the thin walls. Cooper? He couldn't be back so quickly. Nor could his father have found them so soon.

Hadley moved to the door to look through the peephole, and her mind flashed back to the last time she'd done this. A man had burst through her apartment door with a gun and then exited, mumbling about retaliation and taking care of loose ends.

Heart pounding erratically, she peered through the peephole.

A man walked by her door and she caught his profile. Hadley's heart crawled up her throat.

It was him! The same guy who had been at her apartment. He'd found her!

Panic engulfed her and she gasped for breath.

Now...now he would tie up that loose end.

Cooper tried to hurry back so he wouldn't leave Hadley alone too long. He parked the bike and held tight to the Dairy Queen sacks containing burgers. He'd found a small, out-of-the-way gun shop open late where he'd bought extra ammo for the assassin's gun as well. Jogging around the motel to the back strip of rooms, he noticed a suspicious man standing in the shadows.

He'd made the right decision to hurry, then.

Cooper jerked behind a wall to hide. He pressed his back against the siding and found his weapon, chambered a round.

Was that someone for Hadley? Or just a guy out enjoying the evening and a smoke?

Could it be yet another assassin?

Drawing in a breath, he made for the room with their food as though nothing was wrong, gripping the weapon close at his side. In case there was trouble, he didn't want to lead this guy to Hadley's room, so Cooper went straight to his own door and the guy moved, striding toward him.

Cooper lifted the gun and held it point-blank. "Who are you?"

"Whoa." The guy held his hands up. "I'm not the enemy."

"Drop the weapon, son." Ethan Wilde, Cooper's father, spoke from behind.

"Not until you tell me what's going on. Who is this guy? How'd you get here so fast?"

His father squeezed his shoulder, a gesture Cooper hadn't experienced in far too long. "Helicopters are good for that sort of thing. But that's not important right now. This isn't a conversation we want to have out in the open. You need to hear what he has to say. You called me for help. Now, why don't we talk about this inside, and preferably with the girl."

"She has a name, Dad."

"Don't want too many ears to hear, son."

His father had a point. Cooper lowered the weapon, but kept it gripped tightly in case his father had trusted the wrong person. With everything that had happened, that wouldn't surprise him.

God, please let this guy be someone who can help.

Because if he wasn't, he was about to risk Hadley's life…and his father's.

"Here, hold this." He handed the Dairy Queen bag to his father. "Sorry, I didn't expect you this soon or I would have gotten you something, too."

His father chuckled. "No problem."

Cooper knocked on the door to Hadley's room as he thrust the key in. "It's me."

The dead bolt had been engaged. He couldn't open the door.

"Let me in. I've brought my father."

"Coop…you can't trust him," she whispered—or was it more a whimper?—from behind the door. "That man… I've seen him before."

Cooper whipped his weapon around again and aimed it at the new guy. "Who are you? And you'd better have a good answer."

"I do, but I'm not talking outside for the world to hear."

"Let us in," Cooper said against the door. "I'll make sure he doesn't hurt anyone."

Seconds ticked by, then finally Hadley unbolted the dead bolt and opened the door, distrust swimming in her gaze. Cooper waved the guy in with his weapon, and his father followed, a deep scowl etched in his features.

"Keep your hands where I can see them," Cooper ordered. "You have ten seconds to tell me everything and I'd better like what you have to say."

"Cooper, you're out of line here," Ethan said.

"This man is my contact. He's the guy who can fix all of this."

"Let me hear it from him," Hadley said, remaining in the corner, watching the man.

"My name is Lance Gibbons. I'm with the CIA. I knew your father, Hadley. I've been looking for you to protect you."

"That's not true. I saw you burst into my apartment with your gun. When you left, I heard you say you wanted to take care of loose ends. Just a few minutes later, I was nearly killed when someone shot the driver of my taxi."

Cooper fingered the trigger guard.

A bead of sweat trickled down Lance's temple. Was he lying?

He shook his head. "You misunderstood. I was referring to the contract put out on you, the loose ends comment was my reference to my unfinished business in cleaning up this mess before others were killed—namely you. It was a revenge contract, surrounding a mission your father was involved in. I know what happened to your father but I don't know who is behind this contract, though I have my suspicions."

"Why didn't my father give me your name then, if you're someone he could trust? Someone who could help me."

"Did he tell you to call Ronny Pager?"

Hadley nodded slowly.

"Ronny and I worked together. She was killed."

Cooper wouldn't take his eyes off Lance, but he could sense the doubt pouring from Hadley.

"Why me? I didn't even know my father was a spy until two days ago."

"It doesn't matter. They found out that you're his daughter. That's all they care about."

"They. Who are they? How can you help me if you don't know who is responsible?"

"If you know the mission why don't you know who is behind it?" Cooper asked.

"That's where you come in, Hadley," Lance said. "I need your help."

"Wait. I thought you were here to help *me*."

Lance glanced at Cooper's father. "I believe we can help each other. You'll never be safe until we find out who is responsible."

"Tell me something I don't know."

"You are the last one connected with this who is still alive, if you will. Everyone else has been eliminated."

Hadley gasped. Cooper couldn't believe his raw need to take her in his arms, reassure her, but he kept his weapon on the CIA agent. As far as he was concerned, this man wasn't much better than the assassins sent to kill Hadley.

"So what do you want from me?"

"I want to use you as bait."

EIGHTEEN

Hadley was taken aback by Lance's words. His eyes were cold and hard, and she could easily see him giving her up to catch his prey. Her life was not important to this man.

"Not happening." Cooper continued to point the weapon at Lance.

The intensity of his protectiveness and fierce willingness to stand up for her, fight for her, was nearly enough to make her cry. He was the only person in this room she was willing to trust with her life—even if she knew better than to trust him with her heart.

"Let me explain. Let her decide."

"Coop, please put the weapon down, son."

Hadley realized she hadn't been introduced to Cooper's father. Everything had jumped right into the middle of the action. But the tension in the room wouldn't allow for any decent introductions so she'd wait for another day. Hope for another day.

Cooper glanced at Hadley. She nodded. "I think it's okay. We have to trust him, Cooper. We don't have another choice. And he's right, I'll be running for my life forever unless we end this."

"So what's your plan?" Cooper dropped his weapon to his side, but kept it ready.

"Your father told me you had the assassin's phone. Can I see it now?"

Cooper dug it from his pocket and handed it over. Hadley hoped they weren't handing off evidence that could be proof they'd need in the future. Lance carefully handled it.

"What are you doing?"

"I'm scrolling through the texts and phone messages. His contact is on here—this is our link. It's the key."

"Then turn it over to someone who can trace the phone calls."

Lance sent him a look like he thought Cooper didn't have a clue. "I'm going to send a text from the dead assassin informing the contractor that I failed and that I'm injured and out."

"Then he'll just send someone else. Others might already be out there for all we know. What's that going to do?"

"No. This isn't a free-for-all, we know that much. It's just one assassin at a time." His gaze pierced hers, revealing he knew more than he was sharing. "Tomorrow night is the opening night of your exhibition."

"Yes, I was… I was supposed to be there. It's important for an artist to attend the opening, to have face time with the buyers, the critics." Hadley's shoulders drooped. "I know I'm not supposed to care about that right now. Obviously, staying alive is more important than going to the reception."

"I want you to attend."

Her heart jumped at the thought. Could she actually be allowed to keep her life *and* realize her dream? Guilt pulled her insides apart. It wasn't about her debut. It was about catching the man responsible for her father's death. The same man who wanted her dead.

"All right. I'll do it." It wasn't that hard to agree.

"You can't, Hadley." Cooper sounded wounded. Afraid. "What are you thinking? What if you're a suspect in your father's murder? Not to mention, this is your life we're talking about. Is it worth—"

"The law enforcement entities have been handled. Hadley isn't a suspect in her father's murder. If she was, she wouldn't be expected at the exhibit opening night. Doubtful she'd even have an exhibit. The best way to extend her life is to capture the person trying to end it. The reception is the perfect venue to bait the trap."

"And you think that someone will show up there to kill me?"

"If you're there, our killer, or the man behind this, will be there to extract the revenge himself. At least I suspect that our man will be in attendance but if not, then we will snag the man he sends to kill you and question him. Bodies left in rivers or dropped in the Pacific can't answer our questions, won't respond to our methods no matter how hard we try."

Was she supposed to laugh at his morbid humor? Was he trying to make her relax? If anything, his words made her question even more whether she could trust him.

"Now, why don't you eat your fast food on the helicopter. We're headed back to Portland tonight. I'll set you up in style. Tomorrow I'll have a female agent bring you a selection of evening gowns for the reception."

"And Cooper, is he coming, too?" Hadley turned her attention to the guy who'd protected her thus far. She'd go along with Lance's plan, she'd be his bait, but she'd feel so much safer with Cooper at her side. "Are you attending the reception with me?"

But as she asked the question, she realized she was being selfish. It would be better for him to get back to his life, far away from her. In fact, it would better for her, too, in the long run. Life-

and-death danger all around her and Hadley couldn't stop thinking about Cooper, which was dangerous to her heart. She could almost wish it was just the two of them again, her holding on to him on the back of his bike.

"There's no nee—" Lance started.

"Yes. I'm going. I wouldn't miss that for the world." Cooper had cut Lance off and directed his next words to the man. "And you can't stop me."

But would he get his way?

Lance nodded, then looked at Hadley. "Relax. You're in good hands."

Famous last words, those.

Relax. You're in good hands.

Cooper held a glass of ginger ale, stared out the window of the posh hotel and watched the pouring rain. This seemed like some sort of cliché from a bad spy movie. He hadn't been allowed to see Hadley in hours, and for all he knew, Lance had lied when he said Hadley was safe. Why couldn't Cooper see her before the reception?

"I thought I taught you better than this, son."

Cooper had almost forgotten his dad was sharing the suite with him. They'd yet to talk about their personal issues, but compared with Hadley's life, nothing else seemed important.

"What do you mean?"

"I taught you to hold on loosely."

Frowning, Cooper pulled his gaze from the dreary Portland skies and stared at his father. "Get to the point."

"The girl, Hadley. She's got you tangled up in knots. You're too invested. You might try to control the outcome, but you can only control it to a point."

Was this the same man who blamed Cooper for his brother's death? "Who said I'm trying to control anything. I just want to make sure Hadley is safe. Keeping me here, away from her, is infuriating. In fact, I'm leaving now."

He set the drink on the side table and headed for the door. His father stepped in his path. "You know I'm charged with making sure you stay put until game time."

"They should have picked another guard. You're not going to stop me."

His father caught his arm and held him there. "You don't want to do this."

"You once told me that the difference between surviving and dying depends on what we're willing to do. I'm willing to do everything I have to do."

"Yes, but that's not what's going on here, Cooper. Are you willing to live again? Are you willing to let go of the past and hold on loosely to the future?"

"Can you stop being cryptic?" When had his father become so philosophical?

"You're trying to be a hero here and save her so you can make up for what happened to Jeremy. It's plain to anyone who knows you. And… I know that's partly my fault. But I don't blame you for Jeremy's death. Not anymore. I realized that I didn't want to lose two sons. And getting your phone call was an answer to prayer."

Cooper stared at his father, unable to comprehend his words. Once, he'd have given anything to hear them, but right now they came at him in the wrong way and at the wrong time. He let out a defeated huff. "Look, Dad, I'm glad you don't blame me anymore."

But Cooper couldn't just let his walls down, let his anger go so easily. Too much time had passed, and too many things had changed. It wasn't just about Jeremy. Cooper had gone off on his own, building his dream out of reach from his father's constant demands, a business of his own, hundreds of miles away instead of working in the wilderness training business his father had built.

And Cooper had taken his siblings with him. That had hurt his father the most. Even worse, Jeremy had killed himself, while working at Wilderness, Inc., for Cooper. While under his watchful eyes. He couldn't simply walk away from the guilt, even with his father's pronouncement.

"Can we talk about this later? I need to focus on keeping Hadley safe."

"You're right, son, you're right. But I think your past is clouding your judgment. Let's make time to talk on the other side of this."

Cooper nodded and compartmentalized his father's words, even as a place in his heart breathed for the first time in years as the crushing weight lifted. Now, if he could just forgive himself. He shook his head, refocused his thoughts.

"If it were up to me, she wouldn't go to that reception. There has to be another way. I don't trust your friend Lance to keep her safe. I need to talk some sense into her." Ah. That's why they wouldn't let him see her beforehand.

"The reception is important to her. You have to let her do it. You know I'm right."

Cooper closed his eyes, envisioning the look on her face when she realized she would be able to go to the reception, after all. That she would be there on opening night for her national debut. Was her art, her dream, worth the risk?

"Besides, she's the only one who can end this."

"I don't want it to cost her life, Dad, that's all."

"You'll be in the room with her. I'll be there with Lance."

"Anyone else?"

"Probably."

"How much do you trust this Lance Gibbons?"

"With my life. You remember the stories I've told you of my own experience as a SEAL? Of the guy who saved my life? Well, that guy was Lance."

Cooper wished he had his dad's confidence in Lance. He stared at the floor. *God, give me direction.*

"They're prepared to rush Hadley out at the first sign of trouble," his father reminded him. "This is the only way."

"Maybe. But his primary focus is to draw out the man behind the other murders. I wouldn't put it past him to sacrifice Hadley in order to get this killer."

As far as Cooper was concerned, the very nature of being a spy meant a person couldn't be trusted.

"I should never have let you keep me here." Cooper pushed past his father and when he got to the door Lance opened it and stepped inside.

"Showtime."

NINETEEN

This is such a rush.

This crowd was gathered here at the gallery to see Hadley's art and Hadley was beside herself. Moisture slicked her palms as she walked across the shiny concrete floor and glanced at the white walls decorated with huge surreal paintings of animals in a collage of habitats. Lights hung from steel rafters in the open ceiling and softly spotlighted each canvas.

Clusters of people stood around various paintings, holding glasses of punch and eating fancy appetizers.

She touched the expensive necklace Agent Jennifer Shaw, who was working with Agent Lance Gibbons, had loaned her, along with the elegant evening gown and these crazy high heels. She'd planned to shop this week for something nice to wear to this event, and circumstances had prevented her. She appreciated the thoughtfulness of the agents in providing such a stunning wardrobe, though she suspected their efforts had nothing at all to do with kindness.

"How are we doing?" Jennifer asked from behind. "Holding it together okay?"

"Why? Do I look nervous?"

"Just a little."

Well, who could blame her? Not only was this her national debut, but it was also their last, best chance to lure out a killer. All their hopes rested on this turning out well. Was she setting her expectation too high that they would get the man behind the contracts without anyone else being harmed?

Hadley stumbled forward. *Oh, Lord, please don't let anyone get hurt.*

Panic swept through her. Until this moment, she hadn't even considered the possible collateral damage. But she had put all her trust in the two agents—Lance Gibbons and Jennifer Shaw—and in Cooper's father, Ethan Wilde.

"Hadley?" Jennifer nudged her. "Hold it together."

"I'm sorry."

"Smile, someone's approaching. Act natural."

A woman in her late sixties and wearing five-inch heels to go with an elaborate but conservative suit skirt, sidled up to Hadley, expensive perfume wafting around her so strongly that Hadley could hardly breathe. Catherine Bridgestone, an art aficionado and collector, smiled at Hadley.

Say something. Anything.

"Mrs. Bridgestone, thank you so much for attending."

"I wouldn't miss it for the world, my dear. Looks like you've created all the necessary buzz for a successful opening. This is a momentous occasion! I think you're going to do quite well this evening. Your paintings invoke powerful emotions." The woman cupped her hand beneath Hadley's chin and squeezed her cheeks, like a grandmother would do. "You're a bright new face in the art world, one with a long career ahead of you. Believe me, I know what I'm talking about."

"Your invitation was at the top of my list." Hadley hated to blush. It made her feel like a complete novice, which she wasn't, but this event was so important and she was bungling this conversation.

"Didn't your father tell you? I've had my eye on your work for years."

Hadley's father. Blood drained from her head to her feet. Obviously this woman didn't know of her father's death. She should have expected this to come up. The agents had informed her to keep everything secret, including her father's death, for now. The authorities had not released the news of his demise to the public. So far no one had asked why he wasn't attending.

"My dear, is something wrong?"

"No, not at all." The room tilted.

"Would you excuse us, Mrs. Bridgestone." Jennifer ushered Hadley away and over to the refreshment table. She handed Hadley a tall glass of ice water.

"I don't know what I'm doing here. How can I do this, act like my father didn't die in front of me?"

Jennifer smiled brightly and falsely as she urged Hadley away from a few stragglers who started clustering together around them. Through her smile, Jennifer spoke, her words sounding as if they came through gritted teeth. "You're doing this *for* your father, Hadley. You want the man who ordered the death of your father. You want to stop him from killing you."

"And I'm doing a terrible job." But she had to fix things. Hadley stood taller, and made her way back to Mrs. Bridgestone.

After a while, Hadley fell naturally into her role, as she loved talking about art with various potential patrons. She hadn't even noticed Jennifer by her side, but when she had a break, she turned to the agent.

"I thought Cooper would be here by now."

"He's on his way. Don't worry."

And he couldn't get here fast enough for her. Hadley couldn't figure out how to reconcile her emotions with anything about this situation. This was her night, her big night, and everything about it was all wrong. But she kept reminding herself it was for her father. He'd want her to be here, to see this through. And she wanted to find his killer.

She was terrified and excited at the same time. But she also felt lonely, even in a crowded room of people who'd come tonight for the sole purpose of seeing Hadley Mason's art, and hopefully buying some, too. The room felt empty without Cooper. Somehow, he understood her. When he listened to her talk about her dreams she knew he understood. She had a feeling that her father, had he lived, would have loved Cooper.

Loved?

Why would that matter?

Cooper had a past.

Cooper kept secrets, just like her father. She loved her father and hadn't stopped just because he was gone. But that didn't mean she had to love Cooper.

And yet when he stepped through a door and into the room wearing a tuxedo, Hadley's breath swooshed from her lungs.

Was it some kind of insanity that had them all here in this room full of people, hoping that one of them was their man—either an assassin or the source behind the kill contract?

Cooper still hadn't caught sight of Hadley and that made him nervous. He squeezed his fists, wishing for his gun. Tried to look at every person in the room and measure them. Was the man in the blue suit the assassin? Was the woman in the white dress the person behind the murders?

It was even more difficult to concentrate when he realized he was surrounded by the most amazing oil paintings—ginormous paintings that took up entire walls. Hadley did this? *His* Hadley had painted these? No wonder she was making a national debut. He'd seen them on her cell phone but like she'd said, the pictures didn't do the paintings justice.

His father leaned in. "Best to split up and work the room, watching out for any trouble."

"Yeah. I'm going to find Hadley. I don't trust anyone but me next to her." And yet, he'd failed her on so many levels.

If there were someone out there whom he could trust, someone who would put Hadley's life before his own, then Cooper would let them. And then maybe it was like his father had told him. Cooper needed to hold on loosely.

How do I do that, God? Just how do I play this serious game without some measure of control? He walked the room and then…

He saw her.

Standing there talking to a glamorous group of people and making them smile and laugh. This crowd, the elegance, pomp and circumstance, reminded him that he didn't belong. This is where Hadley *did* belong and that twisted his insides. He couldn't fit into her world, even if he wanted to.

He shoved the unbidden thoughts behind him and made his way to the crowd. Like him, the group of men and woman were captivated by her paintings. By her, as a person. Hadley was wrong—she didn't have to be here for her opening to propel her into a national sensation among people who spent megabucks on art.

Then again, Hadley's appearance was part of the excitement in the room.

Cooper had wanted to pull her out of her circle of admirers and keep her with him. By him, safe—where she belonged. Only that was incorrect. She didn't belong by his side.

He stopped. Found himself frozen where he stood staring at her. She wore a stunning azure gown that clung to her, showing off her womanly curves but in the most elegant and appropriate way. Her strawberry-blond hair had been forced into submission, but the color combination of the hair and the dress threw a solid awakening punch to his gut. And the way she moved in those impossibly high heels emphasized the graceful creature he already knew she was. He'd always seen and admired her strength, her inner beauty and tried to ignore that he was attracted to her as well, but all his walls of steel crumbled at the sight of her. If this were any other situation—as in, if Hadley's life weren't at risk—Cooper would turn around and walk out.

He didn't need this kind of complication. But he did need to know she was protected. And that meant he'd stay, despite the risk to his heart.

When she excused herself from her prospective buyers, her golden emerald gaze, accentuated with smoky eye shadow, searched the crowd. Was she looking for him? When she found his eyes, his heart vaulted without permission. Then Hadley made her way to him. He had less than ten seconds to compose himself.

Keep it together, Coop, just keep it together. Don't let her see how she affects you. Don't let her affect you. It's a little too late for that.

Now he was talking to himself.

"Hey there, stranger." Hadley slunk up to him.

This was the same woman he'd watched using Krav Maga against an assassin. The reminder did nothing to stop his palms from growing damp.

"Hey there, yourself."

"Or should I have said, 'Hey there, handsome.'" Her cheeks turned a nice shade of pink. "I mean, Cooper, you clean up real nice. I… I uh…"

"You're not so bad yourself."

That remark earned him a slight scowl. That he'd hurt her pricked his heart. Cooper ran his finger down the exposed, soft skin of her arm. "You're beautiful, Hadley." He wanted to say more, to praise her more, but there were no words for just what she was doing to him right now. And he couldn't go there, shouldn't say those words anyway.

At least his compliment brought a smile to her lovely, shiny pink lips. He swallowed the knot lodged in his throat. What was the matter with them? They had to keep their focus on the dangerous situation. But Cooper wanted nothing more than to pull Hadley into his arms and kiss her. He spotted a dark corner behind an empty wall devoid of spotlights and her paintings. Her art. He'd have to talk to her about that—wanted to know all about her art. Everything about her. But now, Cooper wanted to hold her in his arms. He couldn't believe his lack of self-control.

He slipped his hand into hers and tugged her over behind the wall, quickly twirling her in his arms before anyone was the wiser. His hand at the small of her back, Cooper held her close and looked down at Hadley.

Her pulse beating rapidly at her throat, she drew in a breath. That's all it took for him to lose it completely.

What are you doing? Warning daggers jabbed at his thoughts, but they couldn't penetrate.

He leaned closer. Did she want him to kiss her? Was he overstepping? But the way her lips gently parted and the way she closed her eyes, Cooper had his answer. He eased in.

Just before he pressed his lips against hers—

"Excuse me, Miss Mason." Agent Jennifer Shaw was next to them, hands on her hips.

Cooper and Hadley both startled, then separated.

"What do you think you're doing?" Shaw hissed. "This isn't the time."

"Yes, of course, you're right." Hadley averted her gaze from Cooper. "I'm sorry."

"There's someone who wants to meet you." Shaw ushered Hadley away from Cooper, but not before she shot him a glare.

Disappointment raged inside. Disappointment at the interruption—but mostly disappointment in himself for the way he'd acted. Nothing was more important than Hadley's safety. He was here to protect her, to help her restore her life and give her back her dream. He couldn't let himself be distracted when the person who wanted her dead might be in this very room.

He straightened the bow tie at his neck. How he hated these functions. Why did he find himself in this situation again? He never wanted to be in the position of keeping someone alive, especially someone that he cared so deeply about.

He didn't know how or when he'd started caring about Hadley like this but he felt like he'd stumbled into an abyss and was free-falling and somehow, he had to break that fall. Get back to his wilderness survival training. This wasn't the wilderness and he was doing anything but surviving.

Somehow, he had to claw his way back to sanity.

TWENTY

In a daze, Hadley allowed Jennifer to lead her through the throng. Looked like new faces had replaced others who had already left. That meant more mingling on her part. She'd never thought of herself as an introvert before, but all this talking and chatting and smiling wore on her, especially with the thought of a killer around every corner.

Being here was surreal.

Almost kissing Cooper was *incredibly* surreal. He'd kissed her before—just one quick kiss—but it hadn't been the same as standing in his arms tonight and experiencing the longing and the expectation, the knowing that they would kiss.

If only Jennifer hadn't interrupted them. Not like this was the venue for romance, but obviously the ambience had affected them both. The sight of Cooper always made her heart race. But put him in that tux, and Hadley couldn't think straight.

Had she really only met the guy this week?

Come on, Hadley. You barely even know the man.

But they'd been thrown together in a pressure cooker, which definitely had things heating up between them quickly. She had to catch her breath, get a hold of herself.

Jennifer turned to her. "Are you ready?"

Hadley wanted to wipe her sweaty palms but she didn't dare try that on the silk evening gown. She'd always wanted this—all of it—and yet she felt so out of place.

The agent paused and stared Hadley down, a smile pasted on for the benefit of others. She leaned in slightly. Close enough to speak under her breath and yet Hadley could still hear her. "Get your head back in this game. It's dangerous and could be deadly for you if you don't. I'm here to help you. Tonight isn't the night to be off in a corner making out. You have to keep your wits about you. Now, are you ready to meet Alejandro Castillo? He admires your work and wants to meet you."

"No, not particularly." But if she must.

"Shawn Kaiser, the gallery owner, is talking to him now. There's a good chance he's going to buy two of your paintings. This is huge, Hadley. This is the kind of sale you want."

Hadley wasn't sure why Jennifer cared so much about Hadley's career. But maybe she was simply trying to keep Hadley focused by encouraging her.

"Who is he?" Some people came by invitations, and as word spread, most of the people here were strangers, Alejandro Castillo included.

"He's a real estate mogul in Arizona." Jennifer smiled and continued to lead Hadley through the crowd.

Jennifer was right. If Mr. Castillo and other prominent individuals invested in Hadley, more would follow.

"Now, put on that beautiful smile I know you have, and show him your charming self to close the deal."

Hadley was glad Jennifer was so confident, because she felt anything but charming. She straightened her shoulders and let the heels do the work as she walked toward Mr. Castillo. Another man stood back from him but eyed Hadley. She stiffened.

"It's okay, Hadley," Jennifer whispered. "That's just his private bodyguard."

Mr. Castillo was a distinguished-looking man and smiled when he noticed Hadley approaching. He was in his late forties, maybe early fifties, and quite handsome.

"Hadley Mason," Jennifer said, "Meet Mr. Alejandro Castillo."

His smile was charming and he knew it. He took her hand in his, and she almost thought he would kiss it. His gaze seemed to swallow her whole. "I'm impressed with your work, Miss Mason."

The way he looked at her, and the power that seemed to emanate from him, intimidated her. She couldn't find words to respond.

Jennifer laughed and nudged Hadley out of her stupor.

"Please, call me Hadley."

That charming smile again. "And you may call me Alejandro."

She'd been hoping for something short and pronounceable. "As you wish."

"Tell me, Hadley, what inspires you? Why paint this?" He gestured to her painting of a larger-than-life seal and a combination of landscapes behind the mammal—the arctic, the rocky Pacific Northwest coastline, and a city skyline all twisted together.

Hadley relaxed as Alejandro drew her out in conversation. That her work had caught his attention thrilled her, but despite his magnetism, her thoughts kept tripping over that almost-kiss with Cooper. She'd rather be with him right now, than with this powerful man that could potentially make her career in one fell swoop.

Alejandro had her leading him to each painting and sharing details with him about the setting and her inspiration.

His bodyguard was never far behind, so Hadley should feel entirely safe. And yet she didn't—though she couldn't have said why.

Alejandro gently placed his hand on her arm—the soft hands of a man who had a cushioned life, completely unlike Cooper's strong and calloused hands. A shiver ran over her. She glanced over her shoulder. Lance was in one far corner. Cooper's father in the other. Jennifer was a few steps behind the bodyguard.

Could any of them really help her if something happened?

The crowd had grown with the evening. Why were so many people here? Suddenly, Hadley needed air.

She couldn't breathe.

"Are you okay? You look pale."

"Sorry... I just need..."

"Air. You need some fresh air." Alejandro swept her through a door she hadn't even realized was there. Before it closed, she noticed his bodyguard step in front of the door.

"What are you doing?"

"You need some air, my dear." He ushered her up the stairs.

"But I need to be back in the room. I need my—"

"Don't worry. You'll be back before they can miss you." His hands gently urged her up three more flights of steps.

Hadley caught her breath and stopped. "You know, I think I'm fine now. I'd like to go back to my reception."

The hand against her back that guided her up and forward became stronger than she could have imagined. When she refused to go any farther, he grabbed her arm and dragged her.

Hadley screamed but he clamped a hand over her mouth. He was much stronger than her. But Hadley had her Krav Maga.

Then she felt the weapon jabbed into her ribs. "Don't even think about it."

He shoved her through the door to the roof.

"Why are you doing this?" But she had a feeling she already knew.

He held tightly to her arm while keeping his weapon jabbed into her side. He spoke in her ear, making her skin crawl. "You and I…we have unfinished business."

"What are you talking about? I've never met you before today."

Without answering he shoved her closer to the ledge.

"What…what are you going to do?" The why almost didn't matter at the moment.

"Poor Hadley kills herself in despair over the news of her father's death. Artists are manic that way."

"No one is going to believe that. No one who knows me personally."

"Look at it this way, you'll become a famous artist once you're dead. Isn't that your dream? I'm doing you a favor."

"Can you please tell me what this is all about? I deserve to know that much before you kill me."

He blew out a breath. "I'm sorry, Hadley. You're stunning. It's such a waste, really. For a moment downstairs I imagined you on my arm at all my social gatherings. My wife hates to attend them anyway. The places I could show you in this world. But then I remembered…you are the daughter of the man who killed my son. It has taken me ten long years to track down those responsible for his murder. I am set on extracting my revenge for his death. Your father was among those involved, and you, Hadley Mason, his daughter, are the last to die."

Fear constricted her throat, but she forced her next words out. "I'm so sorry to hear about your son. About what happened ten years ago. But I didn't know my father was involved. I don't even know anything about that." Hadley almost lost her nerve, but she had to keep trying to talk this man down, whatever it took. She would never give up trying to survive this. "When I first met you tonight, my impression of you was that you were distinguished and important, and a…fair man. Revenge won't bring your son back, but will only mean more bloodshed of innocent people."

She eyed him then, hoping her words had reached to something soft, something human deep inside his heart.

Tears streamed from his eyes, surprising her. Had her pleas worked?

"No one is innocent, except my son…he was innocent. Was it fair that he was murdered in cold blood?" He spat the words now, gripping her arm even tighter, eliciting a painful wince.

Hadley doubted his son was innocent if he'd been caught up in an operation that left him dead, but here she was caught up in the same. What did she know other than she wanted to live and she was out of time? "Please…"

"Now, you have to die."

Cooper should never have tried to kiss her.

He'd lost his mind, lost his control with her tonight. The last thing he wanted or needed was a romantic relationship of any kind, and especially with Hadley. She and Cooper were from two different worlds.

Except the image of her standing there expecting—maybe even welcoming—his kiss still scrambled his thoughts. He needed to get his head back in the game and return his focus to protecting Hadley.

Cooper spotted Jennifer speaking with a man next to a door, but Hadley had disappeared somewhere in the crowded room. He spotted his father consulting with Lance. Could they see Hadley from where they stood or had they lost her? Panic gripped Cooper.

Idiot. Idiot. He should never have agreed to this, but the CIA agents hadn't given them choices.

Where are you, Hadley? Cooper pulled out his new cell and texted her. When she didn't respond, he called her instead.

Still no response. Come to think of it, he hadn't seen her with a purse, and he doubted her gown had pockets. She didn't even have a cell phone with her!

He growled under his breath and searched the room filled with what he termed highbrow arts snobs and their second cousins.

"Excuse me." Cooper interrupted a group of fancy-pants ladies. "Have you seen the artist, Hadley Mason? She was here before." Four women rushed to speak almost at once.

"No, I think she left already."

"Isn't her painting vibrant?"

"Dramatic, don't you think?

"I saw her. She and Mr. Castillo snuck away to have a more private conversation."

Cooper focused on the lady who'd spoken last. "What did you say? Where? When?"

"A few moments ago. That door over there."

"Are you kidding?" Cooper said to himself under his breath as he rushed for the door.

He didn't take time to catch his father's or Lance's attention—hopefully, they'd see him exiting. Time wouldn't stand still and wait for them. Cooper feared he's already wasted too much in searching for her. Should never have left her side, despite the agent pulling Hadley away. Was Jennifer involved in this somehow?

Both Jennifer and the bouncer-looking guy—Cooper figured he could even be a bodyguard—stood in front of the door.

"Where do you think you're going?" the bodyguard asked.

"To get Hadley. Where is she?"

"Getting fresh air. Nobody goes up there," the burly man said.

"Hadley would want me there."

Jennifer eyed him, then the bodyguard. "He's right. He and Hadley are a thing."

The bodyguard rolled his shoulders, standing his ground.

Cooper didn't have time for this. He slammed his fist into the man, throwing all his frustration over his past, all his worry over Hadley, into the ball of his fist. Surprisingly, the man fell back, and Cooper rushed through the exit.

He raced up the stairs to the roof, then gently

pushed the door open, aiming to avoid detection in case he needed the element of surprise. But he hoped he would only find them chatting, looking for a moment of privacy. Jealousy surged through Cooper at the thought, but he ruthlessly pushed it down. A powerful and wealthy man had so much more to offer than a backwoods survival expert. At least, Cooper had already cut his own heart out of the equation.

A cold, quiet night met him. The roof was what he would expect of a typical commercial building—flat with fan housings, elevator bulkhead, a water tank and cooling tower. He crept around the structures looking for Hadley. If he didn't find her, he'd have to search the other floors, which could take much too long.

Then he saw her.

She stood at the edge.

What was she doing?

Cooper took a step forward and cleared the cooling tower. Mr. Castillo came into his line of sight. The man held a weapon on Hadley, but he had her inching closer to the edge. Was he forcing her to jump?

Images of his brother standing at the edge of the cliff accosted him. And once again, Cooper was helpless to stop a senseless death. He hadn't been strong enough, good enough to save his brother.

He knew he wasn't good enough to save Hadley, either. But he also knew that she could save herself—all she needed was a chance.

Cooper dug deep into that place where survival was all about how far you were willing to go.

And Cooper was willing to die trying.

Never give up.

"You!"

The man jerked around and turned his weapon on Cooper.

Good. Now Hadley would have that chance.

"Cooper! What are you doing here? You can't be here." Desperation had her reaching for the man who wanted to kill her. "Alejandro, leave him out of this, please. I'll do whatever you want, just let him go."

"Does that include jumping from the roof?"

Did it include that? If her sacrifice would save Cooper, then yes, she'd be willing to give her own life. But she knew the truth.

This mad man set on revenge would have to kill Cooper, too. Except now it wouldn't be as easy to paint their deaths as a suicide.

Grief twisted all the way to her core. She hated that Cooper had followed her up here. His intent had been to save her, she knew—but now he, too, would die. Someone else would die for Hadley.

He was only trying to save her. That was all

he'd ever wanted—and to prove something to himself. That he could be a hero. That he could control the outcome. But she knew things didn't always turn out the way you hoped they would.

What had she been thinking to ever let him help her?

Alejandro slipped his index finger into the trigger guard. Would he shoot Cooper? Surely not—the sound would draw the others.

"You'll never get away with this." Cooper had drawn the man's full attention away from Hadley.

She must use that! She only had seconds to act.

Hadley thrust out her leg, sweeping it up, then down. She wasn't able to knock him to the ground, but she jarred him badly enough that he dropped his gun. He turned on her quickly and pounded her with three rapid punches, sending her backward. She hadn't been expecting his ready response and it knocked her closer to the wall rising up a few feet from the edge of the roof.

Cooper charged into Alejandro Castillo—a replay of their first encounter—just as she plunged into the wall from his surprise punches, and in her heels, she caught the edge of the wall just at the back of her knees.

With the force of her backward momentum, Hadley lost her balance.

She flailed, her equilibrium quickly shifting

away from safety. The night sky scrolled into view as she fell back, a scream erupting, piercing through the night.

TWENTY-ONE

His heart and soul crumpling, Cooper sprang forward and lunged out as far as he could, unsure if he would plummet with Hadley or save her from the death fall. But it didn't matter—he wouldn't leave her, even if it meant falling with her. His hands found an ankle and a portion of her dress, then gripped with all he had.

But Cooper had extended himself too far and began to slide.

Someone gripped his waist. Castillo had been knocked unconscious when he'd hit his head after Cooper knocked him to the ground, but now Cooper thought Castillo had regained consciousness and would kill them both.

"I've got you, son!"

"Dad?" Cooper could almost cry. He gulped in a breath.

But he couldn't celebrate yet. Hanging upside down, Hadley's arms flailed as she tried to peer up at him, the depth of the terror in her eyes whooshing through him.

He heard the sound of fabric ripping. Her dress wasn't going to hold.

"Hadley, your leg. I need your other ankle!"

But with the rending of silk, she dropped even lower and his grip on her ankle slipped.

God, oh God, please, let me save her. Help me save her!

"Cooooper!!!"

The sheer horror in her voice forced strength into his failing muscles. His grip tightened, and he grabbed her other ankle.

"Hadley." He spoke deliberately. Calmly. "I've got you. Remember, Hadley, the key to survival is to never give up. And I'm not giving up on you."

She twisted her torso up and forward, which was no small feat, and grabbed his arms. More arms reached forward to grab on to Hadley. Lance Gibbons gripped her forearms and together, they lugged her form over the parapet and back onto the roof. Hadley gasped for breath, tears streaking her cheeks, and fell into Cooper.

He wrapped his arms around her.

"Coop," she said between breaths. "I thought I was going to die!"

He held her for much too long. Then, finally, he released her, but kept her at arm's length.

He leaned closer, took in her face and savored

that she was alive. Wanted to speak everything he was feeling all at once, but he couldn't find the words.

She pressed her hands on his cheeks. "Thank you, thank you for getting here in time. You did it. You kept me alive. You saved me."

"Do we know that it's over?"

"Yes. He told me everything. He was the one behind the contracts. He wanted to extract revenge from those responsible for his son's death. I don't know exactly what happened but my father, and others, were involved in an operation that killed his son." She rolled her head back to the sky and huffed. Cooper thought back to the quick kiss he'd given her, and the almost kiss tonight.

Lance and his father, as well as other men and women he hadn't seen before, but who were apparently involved in this operation, were now on the roof, handling Alejandro Castillo.

Cooper suspected he and Hadley would need to give their statements to the authorities soon. He held his hand out to Hadley, and it registered that she still wore the heels. Through it all, she had kept them on.

There had been no recording of the conversation or Alejandro's attempt on her life, as far as Cooper knew, but he prayed their testimony would be considered strong enough to see the man in jail, where he belonged. That way, this whole mess would end soon and Hadley could get on with her life. And Cooper could get back to his.

He took off his jacket and wrapped it around her shoulders. He grabbed the collar and pinned her, tugging her close. "You made it, Hadley. You're the strongest person I know."

She leaned close and whispered. "No. Not just me. You and me together. We made it. I don't know about strong. My legs are shaking right now."

Cooper would have wrapped his arms under her legs and carried her off the roof, except Gibbons approached with a couple of other official-looking men. "Look guys, it's cold up here. Not to mention it's starting to rain again," Cooper said. "Can we do this somewhere else?"

"He's right," Lance said.

Keeping his jacket on Hadley's shoulders and a protective arm around her, Cooper let the men usher them from the roof and down a couple of flights of stairs, then into a room with computers and visuals. On one of the screens, they saw Alejandro Castillo, surrounded by men who appeared to be questioning him.

"What's going on in there?"

"Castillo is trying to say you both dragged him up to the roof and tried to kill him."

Hadley dropped Cooper's jacket from her

shoulders, clenched her fists at her side. "He is a liar! He has been trying to kill me for days now. He's already killed others, including my father. You know that."

"Relax," Lance said. "Relax. We have it all on surveillance video and even captured his voice."

Now it was Cooper's turn for an angry outburst. "What are you talking about? You mean you were watching the whole time? You saw that Hadley's life was in jeopardy?"

"Yes, and we were there to help you."

Cooper turned his back on the man. "You have what you need, then. We're out of here."

Two men stepped through the door, flipping badges. "FBI," one of them said.

"You can leave after we get your official statements," the other added.

"Fine."

Cooper and Hadley would cooperate with what appeared to be a task force involving several agencies who wanted Alejandro Castillo.

As soon as they were done, Cooper grabbed Hadley's hand and led her down another flight of steps. Standing at the door that would open back into the exhibition hall, Cooper paused. "You ready to go back in? You must be eager to meet your fans. Except your dress is ripped."

Cooper pushed a torn strap over her shoulder. Her hair had that wind-whipped look. It wasn't how she would normally wear it, he knew, but he found he liked it that way. Wild and crazy.

Her smile was soft and inviting. He hadn't seen enough of that.

"I don't know if there will be anyone left. It's gotten late." Hadley inched closer. "And Cooper, you started something earlier this evening."

"Yeah?"

"I'd like you to finish it, if you would."

He'd already railed at himself for losing control, for letting her get under his skin. Yet how was he supposed to turn down a request like that? He tipped her chin up and gazed into her amazing eyes. Hadn't he known that they were amazing the first time she'd looked at him? It made his gut twist to think that they were eyes he might not see again after tonight. He glanced down at her lips. Lips he might not get the chance to kiss again after they said goodbye once and for all.

He didn't want this to be the last kiss. Didn't want this to be goodbye. Didn't want to let Hadley go. He rubbed his thumb down her cheek and felt the soft and silky skin there.

She'd pulled him out of the mire he'd been wallowing in for too long. That moment when he'd kept her from falling, and knew he would bring her back…that moment had saved him. He wouldn't live in the past anymore. Through her he'd learned to live what he taught—to never give up.

Maybe he wasn't emotionally bankrupt anymore, and he owed that to her. The least he could do was see to it that she got her life back as well—the life she'd always wanted. And that was why he had to let her go. She belonged here in Portland in the limelight. Was it right for him to kiss her without any intention of calling her in the morning? He let his gaze slide back up to her eyes, and saw that she understood.

This was one kiss.

He'd better make it good.

Hadley stood in her apartment. Jennifer had dropped her off here. Hadley had returned the expensive necklace but the dress was ruined, so of course, she could keep it. She didn't really care.

Pressing her back against the door she dragged in a breath.

It was finally. All. Over.

A week in her life she wanted to forget forever. But she could never forget.

She rubbed her shoulders and strode slowly into the apartment, thinking back to the last time she'd been here. How could she stay here after everything she'd been through? But if she left, where would she go? Was it only last night when she'd almost lost her life but got it back again?

And now, she wanted much more in her life than art and exhibitions. She touched her lips where Cooper had kissed her. She'd seen the longing in his eyes and it was the same longing he'd stirred in her, so why did she get the feeling she'd never see him again?

She'd thought she couldn't trust anyone again. Not after the lie her father had lived. But Cooper had been the one to literally catch her when she fell.

Yeah. She could trust that man, even if he had his own secrets.

They'd made a great team, and she cared about him quite a lot. She'd cared for him from the start, in spite of herself, but she'd worried about the danger he'd face being at her side. And yet he hadn't been killed while trying to save Hadley.

I'm not the reason. Not really. I'm not to blame for Mom's death. Or even for my father's.

She released a long, pent-up breath. Rubbed her eyes.

That chair—the one where her father had died—still sat there, stained with blood. Nope. She couldn't live here anymore. Not when all she could see was her father dying in that chair.

A few paintings she hadn't put in the exhibition stared back at her from the walls. The exhibition had been a great success. Everything she could have hoped and dreamed for, sans Alejandro Castillo's attempt on her life. With the media frenzy surrounding his arrest and her exhibition, people would be buying up her paintings, so she'd have to paint more, many more, according to her agent. And just like that, overnight, galleries all across the nation now wanted Hadley Mason's art. Private collectors were already commissioning her, via her agent. Isn't this just what she wanted?

Except, now, none of that meant anything to her. Her dream had come true, and she couldn't care less. The irony!

And maybe she had an idea of what she wanted, but once again it seemed out of reach. First, though, she needed to get out of this apartment. She could pay a service to box up her things and move them. But where?

She slipped out of the dress and tossed the heels off. Dressing up had been fun and glamorous at first, and she'd definitely enjoyed seeing Cooper in that tux. But honestly, she preferred Cooper in his natural environment, in the Wild Rogue Wilderness, where he was a feral creature and part of the landscape. She grinned to herself. Maybe she'd even paint him like the wild animal he'd become the first time she'd seen him, pouncing on the assassin.

And then she knew where she would go.

Now was her chance to finally paint the Wild

Rogue Wilderness, and she had her subject, if he was willing.

A week later, Hadley swept the floor in the old rental cabin—the same one she'd first rented when she'd gone on the run. What would Cooper's reaction be when he found she was living not too far from him?

And how long would it take him to find out?

Uncertainty crawled over her. Being here, seeing the beauty, knowing she would start painting soon, felt like the right thing for her to do. But she couldn't know if Cooper wanted to see her again or not.

Boots clomped on the porch. A sliver of fear snaked through her, but she remembered—the contract on her life was no more. A smile crept into her lips. Broom in hand, she opened the door.

Cooper.

Though she'd just been thinking about him, she was surprised to see him on her porch so soon, especially with a slight frown and not a little fear in his eyes.

"What are you doing here?" he asked, his gaze sweeping the length of her.

"I couldn't stay there, Coop. I couldn't live in my apartment. Not after what happened." She opened the door wide to let him in.

He brushed by her, leaving his masculine scent

to wrap around her. She closed the door and offered him a seat at the table, which he ignored.

She gestured around the bare space. "It's all I have now. Maybe I can bring in more furniture, but this is enough for now. I'm going to put a Christmas tree in that corner."

"So you're planning to stay?"

"I've always wanted to paint this part of the country."

"Hadley, are you sure this is the right decision for you? Seems to me the art world wants and needs you. I would have thought you preferred the city and all that glamour."

"You disappoint me. Didn't you look at my paintings?"

He took a step closer. "I looked. I even bought one."

She gasped. "You...what?"

"It's hanging in the shop. I've started renovating. Adding on. The place getting destroyed like that was the best thing to happen." Pain etched his features. "At least to the shop."

"But you didn't need to spend the money. I would have given you one."

He reached for her. Grabbed her hand. "What are you really doing here?"

"Don't you know?"

He shook his head.

That hurt more than she wanted to admit. "Is it so wrong of me to say that I missed you?"

Cooper tugged her close. Gripped her shoulders and turned his steely blues loose on her. "Are you sure about this?"

"Yes. I didn't like the way you said goodbye. It felt a little like you were giving up. Like you weren't willing to fight for something you cared about. And someone once told me the key to survival is to never give up. And I'm not giving up on *you*, Cooper."

A grin shifted into his lips. "I was hoping you'd feel that way."

He leaned in closer and pressed his lips against hers. Then slipped his arms around her, nice and tight. Hadley let herself melt into him.

This time his kiss held the promise of forever.

* * * * *

Dear Reader,

Thank you so much for reading *Targeted for Murder*. What a "wild" ride that was to write. I hope it left you breathless. When I finished writing the last line, I felt like I had just stepped off Space Mountain at Disney World. I hope you'll come back for Grayson Wilde's story with the next book in Wilderness, Inc., my new series set in the Wild Rogue Wilderness.

I'm always fascinated to see how my stories will come together. I put many hours of thought and preparation into them before I write them, but there are always many pieces that I can't fit together before I write, and some elements I don't even know exist until I'm deep into the story. Many things I don't know about my characters until I live life through their eyes in their fictional world.

Still, so many things just begin to fall into place that it leaves me truly amazed. Not with myself or my process or anything that I've done, but with my Creator. The way my creations come together must have everything to do with the fact He created me in His image and I have His DNA—I create because He creates.

Here is one small example. When putting together the front matter for this story I had to find the right Bible verse. I did the first thing, the simple thing, and flipped my Bible open where it landed on Psalm 103. Skimming down I found the right verse:

The Lord works righteousness and justice for all the oppressed. Psalms 103:6.

Wasn't this the exact verse to also represent my hero? Even though Cooper Wilde has hidden himself away in the wilderness, to a degree, he's really a warrior and all about seeking justice for those who need help and can't help themselves. He failed at that and must prove himself once again. He can't turn his back on those in need. In his story, he wants to take a wrong and make everything right, not only for himself but for Hadley Mason.

De opresso liber means liberator of the oppressed and is the motto of the Green Berets. So the scripture fit perfectly with this story and was just something that fell into place.

Hadley is so close to seeing her dreams fulfilled and after having everything ripped out from under her, she must fight to survive. Sometimes our dreams don't really matter anymore when faced with life-and-death struggles, and then sometimes, we accomplish those dreams anyway because we're strong and never give up. Then we can even achieve our dreams only to realize there is something more important to us.

This happened to Hadley when faced with her own mortality—she learned that she couldn't take God's presence in her life for granted anymore. And that, perhaps, a certain wilderness guide meant more to her than becoming a famous artist.

I hope you related to these characters on some level and perhaps come away from the story with something you can carry with you. I love to hear from my readers. Visit my website to learn how to connect at *www.elizabethgoddard.com*. Please, sign up for the Great Escapes newsletter so you can learn about my next release.

Many blessings!
Elizabeth Goddard

REQUEST YOUR FREE BOOKS!
2 FREE WHOLESOME ROMANCE NOVELS
IN LARGER PRINT
PLUS 2
FREE
MYSTERY GIFTS

✻✻✻✻✻✻✻✻✻✻✻✻✻✻✻✻✻✻✻✻✻✻

HEARTWARMING™

❊❊❊❊❊❊❊❊❊❊❊❊❊❊❊❊❊❊❊❊

Wholesome, tender romances

WESTERN WP PROMISES

YES! Please send me **The Western Promises Collection** in Larger Print. This collection begins with 3 FREE books and 2 FREE gifts (gifts valued at approx. $14.00 retail) in the first shipment, along with the other first 4 books from the collection! If I do not cancel, I will receive 8 monthly shipments until I have the entire 51-book Western Promises collection. I will receive 2 or 3 FREE books in each shipment and I will pay just $4.99 US/ $5.89 CDN for each of the other four books in each shipment, plus $2.99 for shipping and handling per shipment. *If I decide to keep the entire collection, I'll have paid for only 32 books, because 19 books are FREE! I understand that accepting the 3 free books and gifts places me under no obligation to buy anything. I can always return a shipment and cancel at any time. My free books and gifts are mine to keep no matter what I decide.

272 HCN 3070 472 HCN 3070

Name	(PLEASE PRINT)	
Address		Apt. #
City	State/Prov.	Zip/Postal Code

Signature (if under 18, a parent or guardian must sign)

Mail to the **Reader Service:**

IN U.S.A.: P.O. Box 1867, Buffalo, NY 14240-1867
IN CANADA: P.O. Box 609, Fort Erie, Ontario L2A 5X3

WPBPA16R